••• Moontide Fairy •••

Yui Nuir

Argit Lomestometlo

Mimachi

Maiden of the Needle

1

Zeroki

Illustration by
Miho Takeoka

YEN
ON

NEW YORK

Maiden of the Needle 1

ZEROKI

TRANSLATION BY KIKI PIATKOWSKA
COVER ART BY MIHO TAKEOKA

HARIKO NO OTOME Vol.1
©Zeroki 2019
First published in Japan in 2019 by KADOKAWA CORPORATION, Tokyo.
English translation rights arranged with KADOKAWA CORPORATION, Tokyo through TUTTLE-MORI AGENCY, INC., Tokyo.

English translation © 2023 by Yen Press, LLC

Yen On
150 West 30th Street, 19th Floor
New York, NY 10001

Visit us at yenpress.com | facebook.com/yenpress | twitter.com/yenpress
yenpress.tumblr.com | instagram.com/yenpress

First Yen On Edition: May 2023
Edited by Yen On Editorial: Rachel Mimms
Designed by Yen Press Design: Liz Parlett

Yen On is an imprint of Yen Press, LLC.
The Yen On name and logo are trademarks of Yen Press, LLC.

Library of Congress Cataloging-in-Publication Data
Names: Zeroki, author. | Takeoka, Miho, illustrator. | Piatkowska, Kiki, translator.
Title: Maiden of the needle / Zeroki ; illustration by Miho Takeoka ; translation by Kiki Piatkowska.
Other titles: Hariko no otome. English
Description: First Yen On edition. | New York, NY : Yen On, 2023–
Identifiers: LCCN 2022057331 | ISBN 9781975361624 (v. 1 ; trade paperback) |
    ISBN 9781975361648 (v. 2 ; trade paperback)
Subjects: CYAC: Fantasy. | Reincarnation—Fiction. | Sewing—Fiction. | LCGFT: Fantasy fiction. |
    Light novels.
Classification: LCC PZ7.1.Z48 Mai 2023 | DDC [Fic]—dc23
LC record available at https://lccn.loc.gov/2022057331

ISBNs: 978-1-9753-6162-4 (paperback)
        978-1-9753-6163-1 (ebook)

10 9 8 7 6 5 4 3 2 1

LSC-C

Printed in the United States of America

Maiden of the Needle

1

Contents

CHAPTER 1

Spider and Needle

I was fifteen, and all I had to my name was some old clothes, my spider, and a sewing needle.

In the world I used to live in, my name was Tsumugi. Here, I went by Yui. Yui Nuir. I was born in this alternate universe with the memories of my eighteen-year life in Japan, on the planet Earth.

Even as a baby, before I could understand what was special about my new family, I realized that this world was different: It had fairies.

I caught glimpses of them every so often—teeny-tiny fairies in tattered clothing, hurt and sobbing.

In this world, I possessed a kind of gift that allowed me to see such beings. I had abilities of a magical nature, which I learned to control after a little trial and error.

As a baby, you have so much free time and not much to do with it. My awakening came soon after my birth, regrettably. Maybe even when I was still in the womb... It's all so hazy. I don't remember my birth, but I still have the memories of my past life.

Being a fully self-aware baby wasn't pleasant at all. I was bored out of my mind. The people in charge of taking care of me—they seemed to be maids—showed me no affection. I hated having to cry and cry to finally get their attention so that they'd change me or give me milk. They practically abandoned me, which was probably why it took me so long to start talking!

I'll be honest—it also took me a while to realize my new family was nobility, although the fairies and magic had tipped me off that I'd been reborn in a different world.

The furniture was all antiquated, like something out of a documentary about medieval Europe that I'd seen in my past life. Everything was in poor condition. The wallpaper—which had probably been white at one point—had yellowed and was peeling in places. The heavy curtains hadn't been washed in ages and were covered in dust. That was the state of my nursery.

I assumed that my family were impoverished merchants who, for some reason, still employed maids. And I maintained that assumption...until I was around ten years old, when a private tutor taught me how to speak.

I was born to the Nuir family, and the Nuirs had a special power—weaving protective (?) magic in between the warps and wefts of fabric used to make clothing.

The nobility in this world didn't have titles such as baron, earl, et cetera—stuff I'd read about in a book a friend once lent me in my past life. Instead, noble families were organized by ranks, with the royal family at the top.

By the time I was born, the Nuirs were only second-rank nobles. That meant we were just second-best in terms of nobility. Fortunately, this system was pretty straightforward.

We used to be first rank but got demoted back when my grandfather

4

was the head of the family—a fact that irked my father, who bore an uncanny resemblance to a pig. He'd bring up his resentment at any opportunity, grumbling that we should still be first rank.

In this new family, I spent most of my infancy just lying in bed, but I had memories of my past life, and I was totally self-aware. Not being able to move around and do what I wanted was maddening. I could see the pitiful-looking fairies, though, and strands of magic. Learning to control this magic…might have been the one thing that kept me from going insane.

Desperate to be able to do something, anything, I tried using the magical threads to mend the fairies' clothing. When I first reached toward a fairy with the wispy strands, it frightened them. But when they saw what I was doing—that I was repairing their clothes—that fear became surprise, which then turned into joy. When I snipped the magical threads I'd woven, they didn't disappear—they remained in place, sparkling. The fairy gave me a kiss on my cheek and fluttered away, radiant in their exuberance.

I kept using my magic solely for the fairies. It didn't occur to me to do anything else with it. That's how I spent the entire first ten years of my life.

On my tenth birthday, I got a spider and a sewing needle as gifts. I was told that from then on, I was to perform the sewing of blessings, or blessweaving.

You don't normally use spider silk to make clothes…but I figured I'd just work with what I'd been given. Nobody explained that I was supposed to imbue the spider silk with magic. I had perfect control of my magic, and none of it would accidentally leak onto the spider silk when I sewed with it.

I was nimble with my hands, and my needlework was second to none in terms of neatness and swiftness. I'd probably even outpace a sewing machine from my previous world. But no matter how accomplished I might be at sewing, garments without a trace of magic were completely worthless as far as my family was concerned—a fact I noticed only too late.

They had nothing but scorn for me. I was given meager scraps to eat. My family treated me like a burden, deriding me as if I wasn't one of them. The servants delighted in bullying me, a little girl only ten years old.

No child should have to grow up in an environment like that.

A year later, my status fell further when one of my younger sisters learned to enchant her sloppy needlework.

She wasn't that fond of studying, but otherwise, she was a typical spoiled kid—at least, until she got a spider and a needle for her tenth birthday to test her aptitude for blessweaving.

I'd more or less raised her myself, and we got along pretty well. But any kid that young who's suddenly put on a pedestal above their less fortunate older sibling is bound to end up twisted. My sister used to get scared when people bullied me, but soon after she realized her new status in the family, she joined in. Given the situation, I couldn't blame her. Any and all sisterhood we'd had was instantly snuffed out.

She no longer wanted anything to do with me and became even more like our parents: hateful of mental effort, throwing hysterical fits when things weren't exactly as she wanted.

I continued to watch her until I realized something: Apparently, most people couldn't maneuver magic as if it were thread. Nor could they even see magic and fairies.

My sister could imbue fabric with blessings by injecting magic into the wispy silk made by one of the special spiders our family had a pact with. I could manage that, too, if I tried, but by the time I realized as much, I'd already lost interest in doing anything that might benefit my family.

Not that they were worth the effort to begin with. I didn't have a loving

family in my previous life, either, so I started to wonder if I'd been cursed somehow. The most I could do was hope that my luck would turn around in the future.

When I turned fifteen, my family kicked me out.

My beautiful needlework had caught the eye of a certain person who wanted me to work for him. His name was Rodin Calostira; a civil servant, he'd been promoted from third- to second-rank nobility four years earlier.

It was fairly common for nobles' ranks to fluctuate. Exceptional skill and talent were enough to advance to the second rank within a single generation, and families who maintained those exceptional gifts over multiple generations could reach the first rank. That said, even storied first-rank noble houses would get demoted should their talents diminish. That's what happened to the Nuirs.

My father resented Rodin, who'd risen one rank around the same time the Nuirs fell one rank. Of course he hated this man; even a sheltered girl like me knew how accomplished and young and handsome Rodin was. My father was convinced he'd reached his position through underhanded dealings.

My younger sister was very upset when she first heard that Rodin was going to take me in—his good looks were the talk of the town, and deep down, she'd hoped to marry him one day—but her mood brightened again when she learned that Rodin merely wanted me as a seamstress. She taunted me, saying that when she became Mrs. Calostira, she'd work me to the bone. It'd taken just a couple of years for her to turn into a mean-spirited boor. She'd basically regressed.

My whole family was like this—conceited and snooty.

I was at my wit's end.

Initially, I couldn't fathom why my father had decided to give me, his worthless daughter, to Rodin, whom he hated. The reason turned out to be very simple—Rodin had offered a large sum of money for me. One day, my father came home with a bag filled with something jingling. He grinned like an idiot when he peered inside. That's how I knew.

My family sent me on my way without giving me so much as a penny. I was only allowed to take a few changes of well-worn clothes, my spider, and a needle. When the chief seamstress at Rodin's residence saw me arrive, worryingly thin and with hardly any belongings, she almost burst into tears. She didn't ask me why I hadn't been given any of the money her master had paid to hire me. Maybe she'd heard a thing or two about the Nuirs.

Rodin Calostira was, in fact, so handsome that my younger sister's obsession with him was perhaps justified. He was a young, slender man with blue eyes and golden blond hair, so stunning that he could be a model. His home was smaller than the Nuirs', but it was impeccably maintained. I breathed more easily in its tidy, bright rooms. The fairies who lived there seemed happy, which lifted my spirits, too.

Back at the Nuir residence, I'd only seen sad, hurt fairies wearing outfits that were falling apart. Other fairies would bring their friends to me so that I'd mend their clothes. Some hovered around me all the time. It was only after I came to this other noble's house that I saw fairies who were genuinely happy and healthy, and I realized that this was their natural state.

"*You* are Yui Nuir?" Rodin asked me, incredulous. He noted the spider sitting on my shoulder, and then his eyes filled with tears. "I heard you can't blessweave, but that's no reason to treat one's own child with such cruelty..."

I stood there, stunned by his reaction. My new master told me to take it easy for the rest of the day and let me go without asking further questions.

After my first meeting with Rodin Calostira, I was taken to the bath and given a good scrubbing. The chief seamstress gifted me some of her old clothes (which looked brand-new) to wear, and then I was shown to the dining room and served a proper meal.

"It's w-warm…"

It'd been so long since I'd last spoken that my voice came out hoarse and very quiet. I was actually beginning to forget the language used in that world, which I'd only learned when I was ten and rarely spoken in the five years since then. It was no surprise, really, considering my lengthy language delay and complete lack of desire to communicate with my family. Plus, I still thought in Japanese.

"Do you like the food?" Rodin asked.

Not only was the food warm, but it had also been prepared with such careful consideration for me. It was a nourishing risotto, gently seasoned but with plenty of vegetables. A fairy perched on the bowl without the weariness I was so used in seeing in them. They seemed to be enjoying the steam rising from my food, as if the bowl were a mini sauna. That made me smile.

The food tasted like happiness. It reminded me of the one time my private tutor secretly brought me cookies.

"It's…delicious."

I ate with the single-mindedness of a starved animal, but after just a few spoonfuls, I was already full. My stomach had shrunk after a lifetime of malnutrition, so I couldn't eat much in one sitting. I apologized to the cook who was watching me eat, and even this intimidating-looking man teared up with pity.

"No need to apologize. I made this much to see what your appetite was like. I'll adjust the portion size next time, and we can gradually increase it as you get used to eating better."

I was all skin and bones. At fifteen, I looked no older than ten, and both my skin and hair were dull from malnutrition. I was the daughter of a noble, but you'd think I was a traumatized orphan from a refugee camp. It was obvious to everyone at Rodin's residence that my family had not been kind to me. My new home welcomed me with warmth that I hadn't been expecting.

Given the bad blood between the Calostiras and the Nuirs, Rodin's staff had been initially guarded when they'd heard that a Nuir would be coming to work with them. But when they saw that the new arrival was just a scrawny, abused child, they took pity on me.

I liked how Rodin treated me; he provided me a bedroom separate from where I'd be working, and a salary. I was even allowed to have days off.

Back at the Nuir residence, I'd slept in the sewing room and had to work from dawn to dusk every day. The sewing room was quite large, except most of the space was taken up by tables with sewing equipment, bales of fabric, and stacks of finished garments. I slept on a sofa squeezed into a corner, but even that served as another surface to pile clothes on.

I did the bulk of the work while my family members took care of the finishing touches: blessweaving. I didn't know where the garments were then taken, whether they were sold at a market or delivered to customers who had ordered them. I wasn't paid for my work—I didn't even get an allowance—and I wasn't given any days off to rest, either. I had no choice but to do this slave labor, or I wouldn't be given any food at all.

Rodin gave me one day off every week, and I was free to choose which day I wanted.

Just like in my old world, there were two-day weekends. A day was just

about twenty-four hours, a week was seven days, a month usually thirty days, and a year three hundred sixty-five days. Fruits and vegetables were the same or similar to what I knew from my previous life.

My salary was monthly, plus a bonus based on my productivity. I started out with half of what the other seamstresses were getting, since I was just an apprentice. But still, the pay was really good.

Before then, I had never held money in this world, so I had to be taught about denominations and the general prices of goods. I couldn't guess how much things were worth based on the knowledge I'd carried over from my past life. The private tutor the Nuirs had employed taught me mostly about etiquette and didn't mention anything to do with money even once.

Upon receiving my very first paycheck, I went to a nearby town together with a maid who was also off work that day. I was going to buy fabric to make clothes for myself. The shopping district was busy with people going to and fro. We made our way through the crowd and found a fabric store, which was well stocked even though it was smaller than Rodin's sewing room. Its target clientele was people of common birth, so the fabrics on sale weren't anything fancy.

After that, we went to the second-hand clothes store next door. The scraps of fabric they sold were so cheap that I ended up buying a lot more than I could carry home singlehandedly...so I had to ask the poor maid accompanying me to help, even though this was supposed to be her day off. She relieved me of the heavy bundle just as I was teetering precariously, close to collapsing under its weight. "I got this," she said with a slight accent, smiling at me. I was so touched that I burst into tears, no doubt causing an even bigger fuss for this woman.

*   *   *

Back from the shopping trip, I made suitable clothes for myself, reserving the best fabric to make scented sachets for everyone at the Calostira residence. I wove blessings into their lining—a special treat for the first people who had treated me with kindness.

It was the very first time I'd tried blessweaving, and the results exceeded my expectations.

"Uwagh!" I yelped after I transferred some of my magic into the silky thread my spider produced. The fairies I'd encountered had suddenly gathered around me, kneading the magic like dough...until the threads shimmered with different colors. The blessings sewn into the fabric became even more potent.

As I soon learned, a seamstress could perform basic blessweaving by imbuing spider silk with her magic. But when fairies lend their own power in the process, the magical effect intensifies. This type of blessweaving was highly prized. If I'd woven blessings into the sachets' outer fabric instead of the lining, which remained hidden in the finished product, I imagine it would've caused quite a commotion.

The potpourri inside the sachets was also charged with magic from the fairies who slept or burrowed in it.

I made sachets with a lemony scent for the men and ones with a mellow flowery aroma for the women. The gardener had given me cuttings from overgrown herbs that weren't aromatic enough for herbal infusions.

When the fairies saw that I was making potpourri out of the herbs, they did something to bring out a wonderful scent from the leaves and petals.

I was a little worried that the kitchen staff might not like scented sachets, but they accepted them gladly, saying they'd carry them in their pockets that day.

While I wasn't sure what effect exactly the sachets would have, I was

confident that they would benefit both the physical and mental health of their new owners. I knew the fairies' power could do that, because it was only thanks to them that I'd survived on the scraps my family would toss my way. Most children given so little to eat for a whole five years wouldn't have made it. I was terrifyingly thin, but at least I was still alive.

Rodin had rescued me from the Nuirs, and that's why I poured my heart and soul into my needlework.

◆

It was customary for every residence belonging to a noble to have a butler.

A month had passed since Rodin Calostira had taken in the Nuir girl as an apprentice seamstress. Rodin worked at the Royal Palace in the capital, which was more than half a day's ride on a swift horse from his family residence. The king had granted him a second residence there upon his promotion, and so Rodin went back home at most twice a month.

After a month's absence, he summoned his butler to ask about the goings-on he'd missed.

"Mr. Calostira..."

"Is something the matter, Ulde?"

As Rodin's butler, Ulde managed the affairs of his household for him. She was a beauty and dressed like a man. She'd been friends with Rodin since they were little, which was why he immediately took notice of a hint of anxiety on her usually impassive face. She brought him a tray with a small sachet on it.

"Hmm? What's this?"

"Yui made it for you. It's a...scented sachet."

Since Ulde was offering it to him, he assumed the item was safe to handle. He picked it up and sniffed it. His head had been throbbing from

reading too many documents that day, but as soon as he inhaled the citrus scent wafting from the sachet, he felt refreshed.

"Everyone in the household received similar sachets from Yui as tokens of her gratitude for treating her so kindly, or so she said. She spent her first pay on materials for them and made them by herself."

"Is there…a problem with that?"

"I had to check whether the gift she had for you was safe, of course, and… You should just take a look yourself."

She instructed Rodin to turn the sachet inside out, shaking the contents onto a sheet of paper she'd put on the tray. He did so, and dried herbs with a lemon fragrance fell from the sachet. They were infused with fairy energy. Rodin's ability to sense magic was rather faint, but he was sensitive to fairies.

"How could she have gotten her hands on these?! And in such vast quantities?!"

Herbs with fairy energy were cultivated at the Royal Palace gardens in a very small amount. Harvesting them was exceedingly difficult, as the fairies themselves had to point out which leaves had been nourished with their power. Food and herbal infusions made with these special herbs worked as an antidote against poison and also improved constitution. They were a delicacy only to be tasted at the palace on special occasions, impossible for the general public to acquire.

"Master, these are cuttings left after trimming our own garden herbs. The gardener gave them to Yui. That's what she used to prepare the potpourri."

"What…?"

"Yet it is not the contents of the sachets that are most surprising. Have a closer look at the interior."

Rodin looked curiously at the lining inside the sachet. He gasped, stunned.

"As you can see, this is the original blessweaving, which the Nuirs used to be famous for a few generations back."

Blessweaving was called "original" when it involved the power of fairies. It had been quite some time since Rodin had seen any articles made in this way. The fabric lining the sachet wasn't interwoven only with energy from a single fairy, though. It was a rich tapestry of magic worthy of being considered a national treasure.

"But how can this be? The girl is supposedly not capable of blessweaving."

"She is very young, yet she is proud and mentally resilient. Perhaps she concealed blessweavings in the sachets not wishing for her family to discover that she does have the aptitude. Yet another possibility is that she does not realize her ability rivals that of her ancestors. She might not have heard much about them."

Rodin thought about how frail and neglected the girl had seemed when he saw her for the first time, so small that he couldn't believe she was fifteen. From what he'd gathered, she'd been kept isolated and hadn't spoken to anyone for years before coming to live at his residence. She was merely a little girl not used to social interaction. It was possible that, despite being a Nuir, she didn't know the value of blessweaving. Maybe she wasn't even aware of what those blessings were.

"I'm also awaiting a report from Skur…"

Rodin was all attention. Skur was Ulde's husband, working as a butler at Rodin's other residence, the one in the capital.

"You got him involved?"

Like Ulde, Skur was an old friend of Rodin's. He could see all sorts of fairies, even rare ones. This ability was known as faysight. Many a magician wanted him for an apprentice, but he rejected their offers, marrying into Ulde's family and learning the butler profession from Ulde's father. He was subsequently employed by Rodin.

Skur divided his time between Rodin's other residence and the Royal Palace. He would normally have no business at the Calostira residence, which was managed by his wife. She was the more accomplished butler and rarely needed his help—unless it was something to do with the fairies.

"Skur's taking a look at Yui under the pretext of wanting some more of those sachets for your other friends. You might want to consider notifying the palace about the girl's abilities, depending on Skur's findings. The residence is currently blessed with the presence of many fairies, which I can only attribute to the girl being here."

"Ah. I thought I'd sensed strong fairy energy when I arrived."

"There is at least one new fairy here as powerful as the housekeeper's. I asked Skur to come here after she notified me of this. They're investigating this together as we speak."

"A fairy matching hers? A fairy of darkness...?"

A few minutes later, Skur reported that he'd discovered the reason for the increased fairy presence at the house. Neither Rodin nor Ulde were prepared for what he had to say.

•• CHAPTER 2 ••

Fairy Healing

"My, that's rather…extraordinary."

"Ungh…"

I hung my head, sensing more bewilderment than appreciation in the seamstress's voice.

"Oh, no need to feel embarrassed. You look very cute. These clothes do suit you well indeed," the seamstress added encouragingly, making me feel better.

Once I'd finished making the sachets, I set to work on clothes for myself. I fashioned them after the styles I knew from my past life, which I found to be more comfortable and practical. As for why I sewed them in the residence's sewing room rather than in the privacy of my own room… That's because I only had my spider and a single needle, but no scissors or any other sewing implements.

At my parents' house, I'd never handled scissors. My spider made its silken thread on demand, cutting it for me as needed. The work I did there was repairs, embroidery, and other finishing touches, so I hadn't needed to cut fabric. On second thought, it could be that my family only gave me that type of work because they didn't want me using scissors. I remembered that when a garment needed patching up, I was given precut pieces of fabric. Was my family concerned that I would cut up the clothes for sale in a fit of rage? I would never have acted with such malice, as it simply wasn't in my nature—but it was in my family's, and they judged me based on themselves.

Well, to be perfectly honest, if I had access to scissors, I might have been tempted to make slight alterations to the garments I was forced to work on. For example, I could make them look a tad unfashionable or change the fit ever so slightly, such that while the wearer wouldn't be able to tell what was wrong, they just wouldn't feel quite right.

It was only when I sat down to make the scented sachets that I realized it would be impossible without scissors. I felt uneasy about borrowing a pair of scissors from the sewing room and taking them to my own room, lest I be accused of stealing, but I was free to work on my own projects in the sewing room while the other seamstresses were taking a break, so I waited until then.

"I know you do this with the sachets, but…you even cut the fabric for your own garments without using measuring strings?" the chief seamstress, Linne, said quietly with a bemused smile.

"Measuring…strings?"

"You don't know what they are?"

She took a leather case off a shelf and showed me what was inside.

"See, the string with the red markings is for measuring the outer garment. The blue markings are for sleeve length, and the string tied to it is for the sleeve circumference."

Whoa… Who knew…?

"Once you have the measurements, you use these strings to mark on

the fabric where you need to cut it to get the size just right. Everybody does it this way."

I hadn't seen measuring strings before. The work I'd been given as an apprentice so far was just hemming curtains and bedsheets.

So that's what you use instead of pattern paper... It makes sense.

Except this method seemed pretty tedious itself. I wondered if the ill-fitting clothes I'd seen—a terrible waste of precious fabric—had been made by seamstresses who struggled with these measuring strings.

I knew a little bit about pattern paper, but I'd never seen any at either the Nuir residence or Rodin's home. Paper seemed to be used only for books and documents, cut in sizes far too small to use for sewing patterns.

It wasn't until I made the sachets that I realized something: I could cut fabric in whatever size I wanted without having to measure each individual piece. They all came out in exactly the same size. When I made clothes for myself, I only had to picture the finished product, and then I just naturally knew where to cut the fabric.

Even I was surprised.

"Is it very un-unusual that—that I did it…that way?" I asked haltingly.

I was still struggling with speaking, but my voice was no longer raspy or hoarse like when I had just arrived. It sounded closer to what you'd expect from a young girl. People could understand me more easily.

"It's not just the fact that you didn't use the measuring strings, but the overall result… I don't know of any other seamstress who could finish both cutting the fabric and sewing it together into proper garments over break time. You've done it with remarkable skill, too. I don't think there's anything I could teach you, although you didn't know about measuring strings or dressmaking pins."

Seeing Linne so staggered by what I'd done made me feel guilty.

"You—helped me," I told her. "A lot."

If she hadn't lent me those dressmaking pins, or marking pins, sewing everything together would've taken me considerably longer.

"That's not true, but don't worry. I've seen your work before, so fine and elaborate that it made me gasp in admiration. I wasn't envious, no, because at first glance, I could tell I could never aspire to that level of craftsmanship anyway. But I did put in a word for you with the master, hoping he would ask you to come work with me."

She patted me reassuringly, but I was a bit overwhelmed.

"I...I like the clothes you m-make. They look...natural and neat, and... and they're flowy—but warm."

"Aw, you're such a nice girl, aren't you?" Linne hugged me, and we exchanged bashful smiles.

Unlike either of my previous mothers, Linne was a warm and caring woman. The hug she gave me felt so comforting that I wished it never ended.

The Nuirs left the job of raising me entirely to their servants, who were just as unpleasant as their employers. I sometimes saw my mother—or at least, the woman I presumed to be my mother—but the overwhelming smell of her perfume along with her choice of makeup was enough to stop me from trying to approach her.

I was so glad to be at the Calostira residence, with a paying job and this wonderful woman for a superior.

"You keep exceeding my expectations in everything you do. In a mere month, you completed the sewing work I thought would take you half a year," Linne mumbled, defeated.

I worked quickly because I was enjoying it. Everything here was top-notch, from the environment to the sewing equipment.

"Yui, would you like to try your hand at making undergarments for the maids? If you can sew well-fitting clothing without using a measuring

string, I suspect designing something better than a breast band might be within your ability."

"Oh!" I nodded eagerly.

Of course I was eager—most women in this world just squished and flattened their breasts! It was my duty to provide them with an innovation from my old world, one that offered support and stability—the bra!

While we were talking about work, a man came into the room. I'd been told his name was Skur. Four fairies unlike any I'd ever seen before were clinging to him.

Linne explained to me that Skur was employed as a butler at Mr. Calostira's workplace in the capital, that he rarely visited here, and that he was married to Ulde—but I couldn't take my eyes off the fairies.

Fairies generally looked like tiny human women, although they could also possess animal features such as wings and cat, dog, or bunny ears and tails.

Skur had a fluffy green ball on his shoulder, and inside this ball were four kitty-eared fairies snuggled in a pile. They made me think of kittens that'd gotten so tangled in yarn, they were stuck together but were loving being so snug. One kitten fairy was brown, one black, one auburn, and one as yellow as a lemon. They looked very cozy in that green ball, which reminded me of marimo.

Skur picked one from the huddle and held them out on his palm in front of me.

Oh my gosh—is it really okay for me to hold them?!

Without thinking, I held out my hands cupped together, ready to receive the fairy…when Skur and Linne gasped.

"Yui—you can see fairies?" Skur asked incredulously.

"Huh?"

Hang on... You *can see them, Skur?*

I'd been so mesmerized by the adorable fairies that it didn't even cross my mind that I'd just revealed that I could see them, too.

The fairy Skur was holding was dressed in torn rags. As soon as he removed them from the green clump of his magic, they seemed anxious and looked ready to cry. He petted them gently and bowed his head to me.

"I've been looking after these fairies since I found them. Being able to see fairies is a rare gift. Besides you and me, the royal family can see them, as can some nobles and magicians. I've noticed fairies whose clothes have been patched with silver threads. It was you who healed them, wasn't it? Might I ask you to please heal these fairies, too?"

"H-heal them?"

"Ah... Were you not aware that's what you were doing? Well, now you know."

I focused my magic and transformed it into a needle. Next, I unraveled the ball of green magic on Skur's shoulder, straightened it out, and threaded it. I wasn't able to manipulate other people's magic as freely as mine, so I had to do it this way. The reason I chose to use Skur's magic for mending the fairies' clothes rather than my own wasn't that the fairies showed any dislike for my magic; they simply seemed eager to return to the green ball, so I thought it felt good to them. I did ask Skur for permission to use his magic, and he granted it. He reacted with surprise when I made my magic needle, and when I turned his own magic into a thread and began sewing with it, his mouth hung open in shock.

He talked to me as I busily threaded the needle back and forth.

"What to us appears to be the fairies' clothing is actually an integral

part of their bodies, an external manifestation of their power. It is the most delicate part, which gets damaged easily."

I wouldn't have made the connection between the fairies' power and their clothing, but the tiniest of fairies I'd seen wore hardly anything, while bigger ones I'd seen wore dresses. Going by this logic, the more gorgeous the outfit, the more powerful the fairy, I supposed.

"When faymancers steal magic from fairies, their clothes get torn. To them, that's an injury, and their magic continuously seeps out of it."

"What are fay...mancers?"

"Unlike faywhisperers, who commune with fairies and use their powers with permission, faymancers forcefully drain magic out of fairies. This practice is strictly forbidden by law in our kingdom, but faymancers certainly still exist. In criminal organizations, for example."

What...? There was definitely at least one of those people at the Nuir residence! That's why all the fairies I saw there were hurt!

"What...happens when they...lose all their power?"

"They disappear."

Yikes... No wonder the fairies at the Nuirs' were so miserable. Now I get it—by mending their clothes, I healed them.

Skur's fairies, who had been so fearful of being outside the green magic ball, became enlivened as they noticed what I was doing. The three fairies who had been watching their friend get her clothes mended started moving their little hands busily, helping me turn Skur's magic into threads. Thanks to that, the work went as fast as if I were using a sewing machine, and soon, the kitty fairies regained their ability to float in the air as normal. (Or what I assumed was normal for fairies.)

They all now had clothes finished with green thread. Skur's magic worked just as well as my own in healing the fairies. I didn't want the green stitching to look jarring, the mended parts to be obvious, so I embroidered

the hems of the fairies' dresses with a climbing vine pattern. It looked rather lovely, if I do say so myself.

"Incredible. My magic doesn't vanish even though it's been taken away from me."

"Myuh?"

I cocked my head, not understanding. Skur smiled briefly.

"Look."

He took what remained of the clump of magic from his shoulder and put it on a table next to him. It quickly began to shrink, like melting cotton candy, and before long, there was nothing left of it.

"Oh!"

It seemed that magic didn't last long away from its originator, unless it was woven into fairy clothing? And what if it was woven into regular clothes? I had never tried using a thread made from pure magic to sew garments for humans before. Curious to see what would happen, I wove a thread of my magic into the hem of my dress. As soon as I cut the thread, it dissolved, as if melting away. So only fairy clothing mysteriously preserved the magic.

"As you can see, magic normally fades as soon as it's no longer connected to the person who created it," Skur explained. "That's why these fairies couldn't leave my side."

"I...understand..."

My spider hopped down from my shoulder and sat in my lap. It looked up at me intently and produced a bit of spider silk.

I guessed what it was trying to tell me—that its silk could also preserve magic.

"My spider's silk—it can... Magic..."

"Yes, the Nuirs' spiders are special in that their threads absorb magic. They can even absorb fairies' energy."

Was that why my family acted so smug? And they weren't even the special ones—it was the spiders.

"Only Nuirs have this—these...spiders?"

"Correct. Magical spiders are a type of monster, and they're naturally vicious toward humans. Only the spiders your family has been keeping are amenable, but they serve no one else."

I absentmindedly stroked the slightly hairy abdomen of my spider when I noticed something—it'd grown bigger. When I arrived at Rodin's, it was only half the length of my hand, and my hands were very small for my age. It had doubled in size since then.

"Yui, if I brought you more injured fairies, would you please heal them, too?"

I was only fifteen, and I looked like a little girl, but here was a grown man, kneeling in front of me with one hand on his chest, asking for my help with urgent seriousness.

Hwaaah?! Why's this butler treating me like I'm the one in charge here? I'm only an apprentice seamstress!

"Skur, you're embarrassing the young lady," said Linne. "I'm as astonished as you to hear that she has the gift of faysight, but let's not act without due precaution. It could put her in serious trouble."

I sat upright, alarmed.

Trouble? What trouble?

"Oh, I apologize. I didn't mean to frighten you. Girls with faysight are candidates to marry into the royal family regardless of their birth, but you have an even greater talent—you can heal fairies. If your family found out about this, they would be desperate to have you back, I imagine. You do not want to go back to them, do you?"

I shook my head gingerly. The part about maybe marrying a royal one day was a shock, but what rattled me even more was returning to the Nuirs

30

now that I'd gotten so comfortable here. I couldn't bear the thought of being used by them again.

"Do not be afraid," Skur said to me. "Let Mr. Calostira handle everything, and he will ensure that you come to no harm. I swear on the fairies."

His voice was oddly tense as he urged me to agree. I had no other choice but to accept.

◆

I learned a lot of new things that day: that my blessweaving could heal fairies, and that even my ability to see them had the potential to greatly affect my social standing…but that it would also make me a highly desirable target to the Nuirs. After all these revelations, Skur asked me if I would like to broaden my knowledge about the world in general.

Yes! Of course I would! I'd study my butt off if it was to save me from the Nuirs' evil clutches!

Finding out that the lessons would start the next day took some of the wind out of my sails, though. I spent the rest of the day sewing as many pairs of underwear for the maids as I could, and then I went to sleep.

"Goodness, Yui!" Linne exclaimed once morning came, putting her hands on my cheeks. "Your face is flushed red. Are you running a fever?"

"Hwah?"

I'd been very sluggish since getting up, but it didn't occur to me that I might be ill.

"You *do* feel feverish!"

Servants in this house shared rooms, generally with just one person. Linne was my roommate. I was almost done getting dressed for the day, but she made me change back into my nightwear and return to bed. Fairies gathered around me, peering at my face. It was because of them that I didn't notice I had gotten sick.

I'd never fallen ill at the Nuirs', despite the terrible living conditions. Whenever it seemed like I was catching a cold, the fairies would stroke my cheeks and rub my shoulders. I would miraculously recover right away.

It was the same whenever I got injured. My younger sister once threw stones at me for fun and managed to hit me square in the forehead, cutting my brow. The fairies hurried over to my side to lick the wound, stroke my head, and rub me gently. My sister started bawling loudly, scared at the sight of blood and perhaps even taken aback by what she'd done. A maid reluctantly came to see to my wound, but by that time, only a faint scrape was left of it. The maid lost her nerve when she saw it, furious that my sister made so much noise over nothing, but it was me who got yelled at and slapped for it. No sooner had she done it than the fairies were around me once again, stroking me where the maid had hit me, rubbing and licking. It hurt a lot when I got hit, but neither the slap nor the stone had left a mark on me. There was no swelling, and the cut healed without leaving behind a scar.

The fairies would always come to save me from both illness and injury, no matter how minor.

"Huff..."

Something didn't feel right as I was lying down on my bed under the warm covers. My body felt sore all over. It was similar to muscle pain after exercise, but somehow different. I rolled over, trying to get more comfortable, and another kind of pain flared up in my joints. It felt as if my bones were grinding against one another.

"Urgh..."

You don't notice how much pain you're in until you start thinking

about it, I suppose? It really seemed to start out of the blue. Everything felt fine as I was getting ready for the day earlier on. How could it have gotten so bad so quickly?

I curled up into a ball to cope with the pain when the door to my room opened. Linne had brought the middle-aged doctor who had examined me on the day of my arrival.

"What seems to be the matter, Yui?"

"Weren't you listening when I said she had a fever?" Linne chided the man.

"Let's see here."

He took my hand to check my pulse. I groaned from the pain.

"Yui? Are you feeling worse? Hurry up, Doctor, you've got to help her."

"Don't rush me. Her temperature is slightly elevated... Hmm, strange..."

"Could it have something to do with her healing fairies yesterday?"

"Shush, I'm trying to take her pulse. Yui, do you feel any pain?"

Linne was anxiously hovering around the doctor, distracting him. A woman who seemed to be the doctor's assistant gently put her hands on Linne's shoulders and made her step away from the doctor.

"Body...hurts."

I didn't have enough words to describe it in any more detail. Tears rolled down my cheeks.

"It is very unusual for a child protected by fairies to fall ill. Could it be muscle ache from strenuous labor?"

"What a rude suggestion! In this house, we don't force children to do hard menial work! Well, she does go overboard with needlework if I take my eyes off her, but that's about it..."

Sorry about that.

After healing the fairies the day before, I got caught up in making undergarments for the maids. I made two sets for every maid in the household. That was a lot, sure, but it shouldn't have done such a number on me, right...?

The term *muscle ache* did jog my memory, though. I'd experienced something like that in my past life. It never accompanied a fever, so I'd almost forgotten it. Maybe this was...

"Growing...pains?" I said.

The doctor clapped his hands.

"Ah, hmm, indeed! Come to think of it, you are fifteen, aren't you? It's possible now that your diet has improved, your body's started growing rapidly, making up for lost time."

◆

I stayed in bed per the doctor's orders. My body ached, and my joints hurt as if they were being pulled apart and reassembled. Even my head hurt, maybe from the fever. Both moving and staying still were painful, just in different ways.

"Owww..."

The fairies didn't come to massage the growing pains away; they never did when I had muscle aches, either, because that was a necessary part of growing. If the fairies had done anything to stop this aching, it wouldn't benefit me in the long term.

I was making sure to eat and drink well, though. My body, which had stopped developing when I was ten, was busily catching up to my actual age.

I endured massages to unknot my muscles even though they hurt so much that I couldn't help screaming.

Things got so bad that eventually I could barely move, but the entire household looked after me. They helped me to the bath—and even to the toilet. (Ugh!)

Rodin came to check in on me, too. He stroked my hair gently before leaving.

"We'll talk about everything in detail when you're better, but I'm going to take certain measures to ensure nothing bad will happen to you. You don't mind me handling that, do you?" he asked.

Yes, please.

By that point, I was happy to have anyone else but me handle important decisions.

CHAPTER 3

Transformation

Whoa.

Whoa, whoa, whoa.

I was staring at my reflection in the mirror in utter shock.

I'd spent an entire month in bed due to the extreme growing pains, and then it took another month of rehabilitation to recover my strength after it had suddenly bottomed out.

When I was able to, I did sewing work. Sometimes, I found I couldn't move my fingers very well, and that would make me anxious. I was so preoccupied with trying to just get back to being able to move around as before that I didn't even think to look in the mirror to check my appearance.

My hair used to be chestnut in color, but it had turned gray, damaged by five years of maltreatment. Rodin's maids washed it for me when I'd first arrived, and once they removed the layers upon layers of grime, it turned out my hair was actually white. And now it had changed again.

I had the damaged parts trimmed away, so my hair was short but glossy. But it was no longer white.

*   *   *

My hair was *silver*.

The short hair, the same color as the threads of my magic, shone beautifully. It had only looked white because of how severely damaged it used to be.

My skin was also no longer dry and rough. It had recovered its suppleness and smoothness and was porcelain white. It looked plump, even though I was still very slender overall.

My arms and legs had grown to a length more typical of a fifteen-year-old girl (or rather, a petite fifteen-year-old girl), but they were still so thin that they looked as if they might break from a strong squeeze. There were other changes, too—to my chest, and behind, and my waist... Or rather, now I actually had a waist instead of a round belly typical of small children. My body had gentle hills and valleys.

Two little mounds, so small that I could hide them with my hands, had grown on my chest. I placed my hands over them and felt a warm softness. Their pink summits were tiny, but well-shaped. There was something bewitching about them, enticing, as if they were begging to be gently played with. The maids had massaged them for me in the bath, but that had no effect on their growth nor shape, as they remained perky but small.

My waist was so tiny that I didn't need a corset. I already knew that corsets did more harm than good, so I'd designed soft corrective undergarments for the maids to use instead. Women constricted their bodies way too much in this world! Most of Rodin's maids had already switched from corsets to the intimates I'd made for them.

When I lived with the Nuirs, I didn't care about the health and well-being of the other members of the household because of how they treated me. But here, whenever I noticed room for improvement, I did my best to be of assistance.

My behind was bigger than before, although it was still on the small side.

The doctor's assistant said I'd been so severely malnourished that I would've died if the fairies hadn't intervened. She also explained that as a result, any further physical development such as menarche could lead to issues.

"Considering her guardian fairies, this might be rather...*problematic*."

"I'll procure a labyrinth potion just in case."

I had no clue what Rodin, Ulde, and the nurse were talking about... At least, I didn't at the time.

It turned out that my existence was problematic in a whole lot more ways than I'd imagined. For example, the Nuir family's pact with the spiders remained valid only because of me.

These magical spider monsters reproduced without mating. Their pact with the Nuirs suppressed their reproduction, but the moment that pact expired, each spider could produce thousands of aggressive, dangerous monster offspring.

Those who knew about this feared that all of the Nuirs' spiders—except for the one belonging to me, the secret fairy healer—would turn into fairy-eating monsters.

Both my armpits and lower regions remained hairless, either as a result of the prolonged malnutrition or the unnaturally rapid growth. I was told that it was likely to stay that way. Not having to deal with body hair would be nice... I remembered some of the removal methods from my previous life but figured it wasn't ladylike to bring them up.

I'd lost that waifish look—sunken face, thin, dry lips, disproportionately huge eyes—as my skin was healthy again. I had gained some fat, which filled out my face nicely so that my big golden-brown eyes were just the right size for it, and my lips plumped up. They were pink, not because I was wearing lipstick. It was their natural color. My nose was quite low, but that didn't detract from my appearance at all—if anything, it made me baby-faced.

Holy crap. What on earth? I'm a textbook case of jailbait now!

A balanced diet and adequate portions combined with fairy energy certainly worked wonders. There I was, a young girl with hypnotizingly fairylike beauty. At least, that's how I saw myself through my past-life-informed eyes.

The change made me acutely aware that I owed my life to the fairies. It was only thanks to their power that I'd survived, albeit in a nearly starved state, without any physical development for five years.

"..."

About midway through my rehabilitation, the maids suddenly wanted to dress me up in pretty clothes, and I could understand why. I also got the urge to sew outfits to suit my new look.

I should be fine with just a camisole instead of a bra. I bet lace would work for either a cute, sweet look or something more stylish.

I want a lacy garter belt. And thigh-high silk stockings.

Both warm and cool colors would look good on me, although strong primary colors would overwhelm my silver hair, amber eyes, and baby face. I also had a bad association with dresses in primary colors, as that's what the other Nuir women—my mother and sister included—wore all the time.

I noticed my face didn't resemble that of anyone in my family. Were we really blood relatives?

"I...don't look like...my parents," I muttered while looking into the mirror.

Linne and the other maids in the room nodded without hesitation.

"You resemble the royal family more. I think the person you're the most similar to is Princess Soir, who married into the Nuir family five generations ago. She was a great beauty," Skur said, to my astonishment. He'd come with Rodin to see me now that my rehabilitation was complete.

"Ah, yes. Back then, the Nuirs enjoyed a good reputation."

"Soir was said to possess fairylike beauty, wasn't she?"

"Indeed she was. I've seen portraits and bronze statues of her, and Yui is very much her spitting image, although her hair is a different color. The likeness may not be immediately apparent since Yui is much younger than any existing depiction of Soir."

"Kidnappers are bound to take interest in her..."

The room fell silent.

I was right about being jailbait. Actually, I was in even more danger now that I actually looked fifteen, on the verge of adulthood. Even I could understand the appeal of imprisoning me in a silver or golden cage, dressed up like a doll to marvel at.

Hence, it was decided that I shouldn't go out alone until something could be done to ensure my safety.

◆

I couldn't leave home on my days off due to my dangerous beauty—dangerous to myself, that is—so I spent my free time crocheting lace.

My spider could make silk of any thickness or opacity I desired, so I didn't have to buy thread. All I needed to make as much lace as I wanted was a set of crochet hooks.

Without imbuing the thread with magic, I could have it be see-through or an opaque white. There were no other color variations, though.

What I missed the most during the lengthy rehabilitation process was needlework, which I'd only learned in this life. How dreadful were those moments when my fingers would lose sensitivity! With needlework, I could make things of unparalleled beauty at superhuman speed. I was only allowed to do it in the dedicated sewing room, though. Needles are sharp tools after all. I owned just a single needle, so it was easy to make sure I couldn't do any sewing in my room in secret.

When my mysterious illness had proven to be growing pains, Linne gifted me a set of crochet hooks for lacemaking.

I'd never made lace before, but I did have some practice with crochet in my previous life. I quickly picked up the basic techniques Linne showed me, and before I knew it, I had mastered lacemaking. It made me wonder if people had stats or skill levels in this world just like in video games, and my textile-crafts level was maxed out.

It was exhilarating to make fine lace all by myself. The maids I'd befriended praised my skills, saying they'd like me to crochet them bridal veils for when they got married. Maybe it was customary for brides to wear elaborate wedding dresses in this world, too?

That's…that's it! I want to make bridal gowns! Gorgeous ones, cute ones, modestly stylish ones!

With the right materials, I bet I could pull this off!

"I want—to make…wedding dresses."
The maids responded enthusiastically.
"Oh, please make one for me! I will pay for it!"

"Make one for me, too!"

"And me!"

The commotion attracted the attention of the housekeeper, who was just passing by. She had glossy purple hair and charcoal-colored eyes, and she was alluring in a menacing way, like she was dripping with poison. Hmm… Combined with her authoritative air and undiscernible age, she fit the part of an evil overlord's top brass.

Endelia—that was the housekeeper's name—poked her head into the room where we were sitting.

"Find yourselves men who'd want to marry you first before troubling Yui with your wedding requests," she said, then left.

When the maids saw her, they stood up straight at attention, but after her remark, they all crumpled to the floor in a gesture of desperation I recognized from my past life.

"You don't have…boyfriends?" I asked them.

I couldn't comprehend how these beautiful women could be single.

They sighed at my question.

"You see, most of us have cut ties with our families and left to avoid being married off to some ne'er-do-wells. The others chose this line of work because they have passion for it and take pride in what they do. We're all very picky, and we won't settle with a man unless he's decent and allows us to continue working in our chosen profession."

"Ha-ha! And even when we do find a lover, sooner or later they lose patience and make us choose between them or our work."

"Given an ultimatum like that, I'd choose work, of course!"

"As would I! Some men lose their marbles at that and go on to ask if I'm in love with Master Calostira. My blood boils at the impertinence! I'm a professional maid, not a deluded wench hoping to charm the master of the house!"

I could tell that these women wouldn't give their hearts away to men who didn't meet their expectations.

That's the struggle of a top-class woman who takes pride in her career and finds it meaningful... The years go by until she's no longer marriage material, so she devotes herself body and soul to her work. Provided she doesn't land a decent man.

"Happier...alone than with a lou-lousy man...right?" I said.

"You summed it up, Yui..."

"Unlike...my—parents."

"Aha."

"Mm."

"I see now."

To my parents, children were tools. My sister's sole ambition was to get married. She wasn't exactly the sharpest tool in the shed.

My past life hadn't left me with a good impression of marriage, either. I had a despotic father and a timid mother who did his every bidding like a slave. They'd also viewed children as tools of sorts—vessels for their superior (?) genes.

I didn't go to college. Instead, I found a job just so that I could move out as soon as possible and never see my parents again.

My father always yelled at me for not bending to his will, while my distraught mother scolded me for angering him. Having observed their marriage from the front-row seat, I never idealized falling in love with someone the way some people did.

It could've been worse. At least I had good friends and nice schoolmates. Without them, I would have probably never learned to trust people. And without anyone to rely on, I would've ended up as one of my father's puppets, like my mother had.

In retrospect, it was impressive that despite my toxic family in my past life, I didn't let my father break me and grew up to be assertive. At least they

didn't try to kill me like my abusive family in this world. And once I graduated high school, I was free.

In this new world, I feared that if I escaped from my family home, I'd be put in an orphanage or taken in by a foster family. It was difficult for me to find out about the local customs and laws, so I didn't really know what the consequences might be.

"I don't…know about…marriage…"

As long as I could keep working as a seamstress, I didn't mind what happened to me. I certainly didn't have any hopes for finding happiness in marriage. That's what I'd tried to convey to Rodin when he was asking me all sorts of questions while my mind was still hazy from fever. I remembered it when he brought along a man to introduce to me.

Fairies sometimes chose to accompany humans. People with their own friendly fairies rarely fell ill, and they also recovered from injuries incredibly fast. When I'd arrived at Rodin's residence in my pitiful state, even people unable to see or sense fairies could tell that I was blessed with their presence.

But that in itself wasn't particularly unusual. Fairies were whimsical creatures, and it wasn't uncommon for them to temporarily protect a human only to leave them when fancy took them elsewhere. As a rule of thumb, only magicians, who possessed magic of their own, attracted fairies who'd stay with them permanently.

Blessings sewn into garments guaranteed a degree of magical protection to the wearer, which was why the Nuir family had such high status despite their lack of commendable qualities. The spider threads would even catch some fairy energy at times, adding more power to the blessings.

I was lucky in that I had three permanent fairy companions.

There was the first fairy I had healed, who was now dressed like a princess, with flowery motifs on their clothing. Another had rabbit ears, which were white with light-blue tips. This fairy wore a robe that made me think of celestial nymphs, but under the long skirt was a fish tail—so a rabbit-eared mermaid fairy. The third one was purple and tended to hide in my shadow. This one looked like a boy, which was unusual for a fairy.

Other fairies whose clothing I had mended would come and go when they felt like it. Back at the Nuir residence, they would only come when I was alone. Even my three regular fairies hid whenever someone was around. Here, though, they soon felt at ease with the members of the household. They seemed to have taken a liking to the maids and would hover around them when they were near me.

I could see clearly now that something was very wrong with my family's house, full of injured fairies. I told Rodin and Skur that I suspected a faymancer lived there. I used to think that the fairies I had helped were bringing their friends to me from far and wide so that I could mend their clothes, too, but that couldn't explain the sheer number of fairies in need of help. Since coming to Rodin's residence, I hadn't seen a single injured fairy besides the ones Skur had taken into his care and brought to me for healing.

Skur, who knew about the fairies' behavior because of his faysight, told me that they didn't normally hide from humans who couldn't see them, although they avoided people they disliked.

There was definitely something off about the Nuir residence. I tried explaining this as best I could.

"I see...," Skur said.

He smiled at me, as did Rodin. The hint of menace in their smiles made me feel glad that they were on my side.

Not long after my fairies grew accustomed to life in the new house and I recovered my strength and returned to work, Rodin summoned me to the guest room and introduced me to someone.

◆

Ewww, are you serious?

That was my first thought when I saw the man Rodin wanted me to meet.

He was handsome; there was nothing wrong with the man per se. His hair was a deep blue, and his eyes were amber like mine. He sported a goatee and was muscular but slim (I guess you'd call that an athletic build), with long, slender limbs—like one of those classy models. He reminded me of famous actors from my past life, of the mischievous-playboy-getting-on-in-years type. The fact that he was a rather fine specimen made this all the more tragic.

Somber black with gaudy ultramarine... Actually, the color palette wasn't even the worst of it. But everything else, from the cut of his clothes to the quality of the stitching, made me want to scream.

"Yui, meet our former king."

I was so appalled by what the guest was wearing that I didn't register what Rodin was saying to me. Whoever made this man's clothes must have been out of their mind. It was a crime to put such ill-designed garments on this well-proportioned, debonair man!

"Please take—take your clothes...off!"

Right. What a fine first impression I was making. Me, a young girl, asking an older man to undress before even saying hello.

"These clothes are...not fit...for wearing!" I clumsily pleaded as the two men stared at me, wide-eyed.

Maybe this was some strange fashion popular among high society, but I didn't care—that outfit has *got* to go!

"Really? Are they so hideous?"

Our guest's surprised expression was actually pretty charming for a man his age, but he certainly didn't have an eye for fashion.

His garments had fancy gems sewn in random places all over— extremely tacky. But since he was so well-groomed and distinguished, he could at least pass for a commoner at best.

As a high-level seamstress (if I do say so myself), I recognized that the fabric and embellishments were high quality and no doubt very expensive. If he could afford that, why not hire a better seamstress?

"Allow me to…make you…new clothes!"

I'll be your ticket to first-class needlework!

The two men got caught up in my excitement and let me lead them to the sewing room. Our guest took off his tunic and handed it to me with an amused look on his face.

When I saw what he was wearing underneath, not to mention his pants (which had been covered up by the ridiculously long tunic), I nearly had a stroke. That's how awful they were.

"Yui, for now, limit your alterations to this garment. I can see that you want our guest to take off his pants and undergarments, too, but for good-ness' sake, understand that this is not appropriate…"

Rodin sounded pained as he spoke to me, rubbing his temples as if try-ing to relieve a headache.

I took the tunic with barely hidden disgust and examined it. It had a belt at waist height, but it was so long, it awkwardly ended below the man's knees. I looked from him to the tunic and estimated that when he had it on, the bottom hem was only fifteen centimeters from the ground. Even if it was supposed to be in the style of a magician's robe, it revealed the man's ankles and a part of his shin at that length, which by any standards was cringey.

Even more ridiculously, the tunic was made like a tube, with the front

and back pieces exactly the same. While the belt helped somewhat, it couldn't have been comfortable to wear.

The two men quietly watched as I picked up a pair of scissors. I was going to start by trimming the tunic's hem...only to find that I couldn't cut it.

Clang!

The blades of the scissors bounced off the fabric.

"Huh?"

"Yui, this garment has blessings sewn in. It repels all blades," Rodin informed me with a strained smile.

"Blessings...sewn in this?"

"It has long been a custom for the kings to exclusively wear blessed clothes made by the Nuir family."

"This man...is a king?"

"Ah, I'd suspected you weren't paying attention when I introduced His Highness. This is Argit Lomestometlo, the former king."

"Oh..."

Well, that was a surprise.

He'd taken off his tunic for me without any complaint. That must have been either because he trusted Rodin or because he was so self-assured as a former king that he was willing to let a clueless, pitiful-looking girl see for herself that his tunic couldn't be cut.

"I'm Yui...a seamstress."

I introduced myself, lifting the hem of my skirt and curtsying. I should've introduced myself earlier, but I'd been too distracted by his awful clothes...

That was my bad.

Although, I was far more distressed by not being able to do anything about his horrible attire.

Just as I was racking my brain on a work-around for being unable to cut the fabric, the boyish fairy stepped out of my shadow and unsheathed a rapier. They stabbed the tunic with the sword. I'd never seen them take that out before, so I'd assumed it was purely decorative. Apparently, it wasn't.

"What in the world...?!" Argit's eyes were as wide as saucers as he watched my fairy.

I thought he was being cute for a middle-aged man. I picked up the tunic again and saw that the severed threads of blessings had lost all their power. Their ends were dangling from the raw edge of the fabric pitifully.

"Wow..."

My fairy flashed me a proud smile (which was super adorable, given their tiny size), gave me a thumbs-up, and disappeared into my shadow again. I applauded their excellent work.

"What...? How is that possible?! How did that fairy do it?!" Argit exclaimed.

"Um...what happened, exactly?" Rodin asked him. "The blesswoven garment has been cut somehow?"

Paying the men no heed, I laid out the cut pieces of fabric and ornaments, which had fallen onto the worktable, and then I reached for the scissors again.

"Yui? Ah, she's not listening."

"What is she going to do with those scissors?"

I could perform blessweaving. While I knew revealing I had that talent might complicate my life, the men were already aware of the fact that I possessed faysight, that fairies favored me, and that one of my companions was a boyish fairy with a potentially very dangerous ability.

I chose to trust Rodin, who was held in high regard by everyone in his household. I chose to trust the former king Argit, whom Rodin had brought to his residence to meet me.

I would display the full extent of my skills for them.

My main motivator, though, was outrage. Outrage over how this poor man had to wear such dingy clothes purely for the blessings sewn within them!

Meanwhile...at the "Superior" Nobles' House

Clatter! Smash!

Someone was breaking everything in sight in a fit of rage.

"Curse that snotty upstart!"

House Nuir was comprised of nobles in the artisan category. As the only family who could imbue garments with the power of the fairies via blessweaving, in this land where the bond between fairies and humans was highly cherished, they had a special status—and were closely affiliated with the royal family's founder.

The Nuirs were, in fact, descended from one of the royal princesses. She was the one who'd made a pact with the spiders, giving the Nuir bloodline their unique ability. The Realm Weaveguardian—who was the weaver of the enchanted barrier around the kingdom, ensuring that only a limited, or safe, amount of magic could exist within—also had a connection to the Founder, the first of the Nuirs.

"How dare he insult us, a first-rank family by *right*!"

The nobles were divided by ranks. There were seven ranks in total. The

Nuir family started out at the first—top—rank, but they had since fallen to third rank. The previous head of the family had made wrong business decisions, which led to them losing half of their land. Around the time Yui was born, they were demoted to second rank and had recently fallen to third rank on account of their failing level of skill, an embarrassment for artisan-class nobility. Yet they didn't see that they only had themselves to blame for this state of affairs.

They'd rid themselves of their worthless older daughter in exchange for a hefty amount of money, but the man who employed her was Rodin, a young and promising aristocrat whom they despised out of envy.

Yui's father yelled and broke things until his anger subsided. Then he grinned.

Rodin was a capable man of great talent, and he'd single-handedly raised his family's standing from fourth rank to second. People speculated that the only reason he hadn't made it to first rank was the humble origins of his family, who did not have a drop of royal blood in them.

While Yui had no special ability and was so emaciated that she looked as if she had one foot in the grave, she was of the Nuir bloodline. Had she inherited the blessweaving ability, she'd have been made the head of the household one day.

"Hmph! I see through your schemes, Rodin! You lied that you wanted her only for her needlework, but your real intention was to wed a Nuir so that you could further advance in rank!"

He took out a piece of parchment from his inner breast pocket. It calmed him to look at it. It was a written pact, which, among other things, stated that when a Nuir was married off to another family, it was the head of the Nuir family's duty to reassign their spider to someone else. This was to prevent the proliferation of the creatures, which carried considerable risks.

Yet Yui's father hadn't canceled Yui's pact with her spider. Neither had he given her any advance warning.

Their spiders were monsters known to greedily devour both fairies and humans alike. The Nuirs suppressed the spiders' natural bloodthirstiness through their pact with them.

"Heh-heh-heh... The moment she changes her family name, her pact will become invalid. There will be nothing stopping her spider from attacking Rodin and the rest of his rotten household."

He laughed maniacally. A spider the size of an adult human scuttled out from behind a woman sitting in the corner of the room, a slave's collar on her neck. The spider made creaky noises as if it were laughing along with the man.

◆

"The quality is not as good as it used to be? The needlework is poor? Nonsense! How dare they slander us!"

The slave woman awoke to her stomach being kicked.

Not this again.

Hearing the monstrous squeals of her present master, she turned her face toward the sound. She was almost completely blind.

The kicking didn't hurt that much. The man's legs were short and fat, his body unaccustomed to exercise, and his aim poor. It was far worse when he crushed her hands by stepping on them, putting his whole weight into it.

"Argh... Ahhh!"

"Blessweaving is the special ability of the Nuirs and no one else! But these threads? They barely have any magic in them! Steal more from the fairies—what do you think I'm keeping you for?!"

He'd stomped on her hands, now bloody and bruised, at every opportunity, perhaps because her vacant-eyed reactions pleased him somehow. But there was no sound of fingers breaking this time.

The woman was a faymancer. However, she had very little power, and her master had sold her when the opportunity presented itself. She could only attract fairies but not steal power from them. This ability was, in fact, very unusual among faymancers, who were generally repulsive to the fairies.

When her earlier master first discovered what she could do, he was over the moon. She seemed like a prized find. He'd come across her in a village where he was hunting for fairies. The villagers despised faymancers, but she—a simple girl whose parents were poor farmers—fell in love with the handsome faymancer from the city who told her she was special, and so she eloped with him.

Thus, she had sealed her fate.

If only he had not found her.
If only she had been discovered by a magician rather than a faymancer.
If only she had cared more about the fairies.

Her life could have been so different...

*　　*　　*

Her power wasn't limitless.

Neither she nor the faymancer considered fairies autonomous creatures. To them, they were resources to be exploited without a second thought.

But fairies did have their own minds and their own will. They learned who their enemies were and fled from them. The girl could only attract them for three, maybe four years at most until all the fairies in the area became wise to what she and her companion wanted to do to them. They would desert the area. Few new fairies would be born there, and eventually, there would be no more fairies to be found in that area.

Consequently, the woman's value to her master drastically decreased. Eventually, the man she loved sold her into slavery. She was passed from one faymancer to the next, used as a lure for fairies for as long as it worked. She could only lament her fate.

Why do I have to suffer like this? All I wanted was to be happy...

"Will I have to pay yet another ridiculous sum to hire a new faymancer? Damn it all!"

Her master's shouting pierced her ears. She followed him with her empty eyes as he stormed out of the room.

She thought of her first master, the man she still loved.

Creak... Crrreak...

The spider behind her was making noises.

*　　*　　*

"Heh-heh-heh-heh…"

Not sensing even one last remnant of fairy magic around, the spider began feeding on the girl's own energy. Unlike her, it was highly accomplished at manipulating magic.

A thought sprung into the woman's mind, that her master would surely bring her beloved faymancer to the residence.

"Ah-ha-ha-ha!"

And she would then devour him.

She'd gained the spider's ability to drain magic power from other creatures. At long last, she became a faymancer in name and in essence.

Thinking of how delicious he would be—a faymancer who preyed on fairies—she began to salivate.

I'll consume every last bit of him…

He'll become a part of me forever.

And then—finally—I will find bliss.

The spider clambered onto her back, and its abdomen began fusing with her body.

CHAPTER 4

Maiden of the Needle

Working with expensive fabric was no different from working with any I'd used before. The tunic was unnecessarily long and wide, like the shirts older men in my previous world liked to wear when golfing. Perhaps it had been fashioned out of some kind of sack? In any case, I easily trimmed it down and remade it into a classic button-up shirt.

"So quick…," muttered Argit, watching me, transfixed.

I was sewing with a standard thread. The threads the sword-bearing fairy had cut were spider silk, and I didn't want to risk him jumping out again to destroy what I was making. He probably wouldn't do such a thing, but it wasn't a risk I considered worth taking—it would be highly unprofessional should such an accident happen.

"Please…try it on?"

I was fairly sure I got the fit right, but I wanted to hear the opinion of the person who'd be wearing it. Argit carefully took the garment from me and put it on.

"Well, well… Color me surprised. I had no idea that ordinary clothes could be so comfortable."

"The garments Yui makes are far from ordinary, Your Highness. She is a top-class seamstress, and the clothes she crafts are accordingly the finest there are, even when they lack blessings. The tunic you were wearing had been blesswoven, but that was its only redeeming quality. Any seamstress worth a dime would be appalled by it."

Harsh, but fair. It was worse than a child's first attempt at hemming a dustcloth!

"Is…it tight…anywhere? Diffi—cult to move in?"

Argit looked at me with an almost tearful expression.

"You will have to forgive me, for I have only ever known garments that were tight and constricting to the point of being painful to wear. As such, I simply cannot think of anything you might improve on. This shirt is the most comfortable item I have ever worn, so much so that I'm finding the vest underneath to be most disagreeable."

"Your Highness…"

"…"

Oh, my heart! Poor Argit! The once and former king, relegated to subpar clothes—how sad!

The next thing I knew, my eyes brimmed with tears. Even Rodin was rubbing his eyes, sniffling.

"Yui, please outfit His Highness with more appropriate clothing posthaste."

"Yes, Master Rodin!" I replied.

Rodin was likewise overcome with pity. Ulde and Skur appeared unexpectedly with bales of high-quality fabric.

"Could you also make a gown for His Highness like the one you made for me?"

Maiden of the Needle

I nodded, understanding that Rodin wanted me to weave blessings into it as well. He meant a yukata. I'd made one for Rodin sometime earlier, and he had taken a great liking to it. Yukata were easy to make, being cut from a single piece of fabric. Rodin was using his as a dressing gown after taking a bath, and he seemed to have developed an appreciation for how comfortable and easy to wear it was.

It did take me some time to make a set of day wear for the former king, though, comprising both outerwear and undershirts.

I left the pricey, heavy fabrics on the side and selected lightweight, breezy ones for the undergarments. I laid them out on the worktable, cutting them swiftly, every snip of my scissors as accurate as could be. After stitching the pieces together, I gently rubbed my spider's back. It instantly spun silk for me, which I threaded through my needle.

"Your Highness has good affi-affinity with fairies of light, ice, sky, and moon. And—green fairies," I said quietly, noticing the types of fairies who had gathered around us. For some reason, they were all very tiny.

"Will you please...help?" I asked them gently, not wishing to pressure these small fairies. I just wanted the ones who were willing and able to spare a little of their power to come forward and assist me.

Argit Lomestometlo, the former king, gasped in astonishment. He was already quite shocked to find that Rodin's residence was inhabited by numerous fairies, all in perfect health—something you'd normally only see in places designated as sacred. What blew him away even more, though, was the skill of this Nuir girl, whom he'd been told ought to be the head of her family instead of her father.

Fairies were dancing on top of Yui's spider, twirling around and hopping off to let another one have their turn. There was a little crowd of them gathered around, waiting to impart some of their power to the thread. Argit had to fight the urge to rub his eyes—so unbelievable was this scene.

Normally, blessweaving worked differently—the seamstress imbued the thread with her own magic, hoping that wisps of magic from nearby fairies would stick to it, too. It was extremely uncommon for fairies to willingly take part in blessweaving. Having them line up eagerly waiting to lend their power was nothing short of a miracle.

"For this part...could the moon fairies...help?" Yui asked quietly.

Lo and behold, the fairies reorganized themselves, and different ones came forward.

Argit was dumbstruck. Magicians could get fairies to listen to their orders, but they needed to infuse their words with magic for the fairies to pay them any mind, and the fairies had to be in the mood to do them a favor. This young girl was not a magician, and yet fairies had come to her assistance, happily offering up their magic.

She didn't just deserve to be the head of her family. She was on par with its legendary Founder. Her craftsmanship was extraordinary, too—she'd cut fabric without measuring, stitch pieces together so swiftly that it seemed like magic, and make clothes in designs Argit had never seen before in his life.

"This here...nightgown."

She took out a smaller version from her clothes chest, brought to her by Ulde, to show him how to wear this unusual garment.

"Try...like this."

Yui turned away from him, slipping out of her dress and into the gown. He noted how charmingly petite she was.

Argit stripped naked and put on the gown the way Yui had demonstrated.

He closed his eyes and reveled in the sensation. He felt the weariness that had been his inseparable companion fade away for the very first time.

"Wonderful…"

He noticed a change in his own fairies. Their red baby dresses had transformed into miniature versions of the gown he was wearing, though in more vibrant colors. They seemed to have evolved from babies into toddlers. Argit had heard of this extraordinary phenomenon sometimes occurring when a magician's power suddenly increased.

"Your Highness," Rodin said in awe, "your magical aura is different…"

Argit nodded. Even Rodin, who couldn't see fairies, had sensed their transformation.

"I see now why you insisted on introducing me to this young lady."

"Even I had no idea about the true extent of her abilities…"

Yui cocked her head, looking at them as if she didn't understand why they were so astonished.

◆

Argit literally glowed in his new yukata. He was radiant, and his yukata shimmered so brightly that I had to squint to look at him. There was a lot of moon, water, and ice energy, and the light energy kind of diffused everything… The silvery-blue magic from the yukata filled the room, making the air feel lighter and purer.

"I see now why you insisted on introducing me to this young lady."

"Even I had no idea about the true extent of her abilities…"

I heard their surprised voices, but I was too mesmerized by the magical glow to pay them much attention. My retinas were starting to burn.

Not only that, but Argit's fairies had also evolved. Their dresses looked like yukata now—they must have been influenced by what he was wearing. And that's not all: He was so stunning once he had properly made clothes on. I was entranced as if I'd come face-to-face with my favorite movie star of all time. Which was quite an upgrade from my initial impression of him as just some actor I knew about but wasn't really into.

I guess you could call this a glow up?

Uuuugh, a simple shirt and slacks would suit him just fine, but now I'm dying to dress him in a military uniform! A black one, and a white one, and one to match the energy of his fairies and his magic: sky blue and indigo! Add in some silver embroidery, some gold thread accents...

My creative urges had consumed me.

He'd look fantastic dressed up smart, but he'd pull off a casual look just as well. Or even if he just had his uniform draped over his shoulders...

This fantasy world is ready for that, isn't it? I'm free to use the fabric Ulde and Skur brought me any way I want, right?

To start with, I made Argit a set of shirts, pants, and underwear. His boots at least appeared to have been made by a top-notch shoemaker... But lace-up boots didn't go well with a yukata, so I made him a pair of zori sandals woven from strips of cloth, with blessings sewn into the toe strap and the edges.

I'd once made decorative fabric zori in my past life, but this was the first time I'd made ones intended for actual use.

"With the gown...wear these. Instead of—boots."

"Oh? This footwear doesn't seem to offer much protection from the elements."

I worried for a moment that he wasn't going to even try them on, but he sat on a chair Ulde offered him, removed his tall boots, and slid his feet into the sandals. Then he beamed in delight.

"Ah, yes… Very comfortable."

I was still a little nervous as to how he'd take to the novelty of sandals.

Rodin smiled smugly. "I daresay the protection offered by the sewn-in blessings is worth more than having better coverage."

"My feet do get disagreeably sweaty in boots. They're unnecessarily heavy, too."

Argit's complaint triggered memories from my past life, as well as the realization that now I could create garments of my dreams.

"I can…make your boots more c-comfortable. By adding…fabric with blessings."

Something moisture-wicking, deodorizing.

My needle wasn't suitable for embroidering leather, but I could weave blessings into his laces to make the boots lighter and to give them defensive properties.

I would've liked to ask the artisan who'd made his boots for permission before making such alterations, though.

"You can? Really?"

He beamed at me—by which I don't mean that he just smiled widely; he *literally* radiated light. This was now the second time in one day.

"Oh, my apologies. My magic is a little overactive at the moment."

I was still squinting from the brightness when he suddenly picked me up and sat me down on his knees.

Whoa, whoa, whoa! Is this even allowed? A humble seamstress sitting in the former king's lap?

…No one's saying anything, so I guess it's no big deal?

"Yui, haven't you been overusing your magic? You've done quite a lot of blessweaving today…"

"Huh?"

Argit must have noticed how flustered I was; he sounded concerned.

I cocked my head at him. All I'd done so far was just sew blessings into his yukata and zori.

There were so many things I didn't know at the time. For one thing, people who performed blessweaving didn't usually have magic of their own, and it would take them many days to complete a single garment. Or that in my case, I had an inexhaustible supply of magic for sewing.

I'd been offered a cup of tea, which I accepted, still seated in Argit's lap.

"Take a break," Argit urged me.

"Buh?"

But I'm not tired. Like, at all.

"The amount of work you've done should've taken you a whole day."

"Really?"

"And I'm basing that estimate on the finest seamstresses in your family's heyday. Now I can't imagine your family taking less than three years to produce anything comparable." He then muttered under his breath that the other Nuirs seemed to lack even the most basic sewing skills, too.

I had to agree with him there. Actually...that awful getup Argit came in wearing—was that my father's work? Was he so incompetent a seamster that it'd taken him three years to make *that*?! I can't believe we're related! How embarrassing!

"What? Three years?" Rodin couldn't believe what he was hearing.

"By the way, Rodin—the Nuir family has been strangely interested in you," said Argit.

"Yes. It seems they begrudge me for getting promoted to a higher rank around the time theirs dropped. Despite the two being completely unrelated."

"You're very fortunate to have got Yui from them."

72

They were probably so desperate for money that they'd given me away without a second thought. I could tell my mother and father had been struggling financially.

"Very fortunate indeed. Yui, may I ask you something?"

"Myuh?"

"Why did you never show your family that you could blessweave? You'd have escaped that dreadful abuse."

Ah... Of course he'd wonder about that.

The reason for my family's current low standing was that my inability to blessweave had become public knowledge.

Girls born to aristocratic families normally made their high-society debut at the age of twelve. I didn't, because my family made it clear that I was an embarrassment unworthy of the Nuir name. From then on, I was doomed to a life of servitude to the Nuir family...

Thank goodness Rodin took me under his wing. Was it because I distinguished myself with my skillful needlework? The Nuirs had no use for even the most talented seamstress if she couldn't blessweave.

Based on the current conversation, though, the Nuirs loathed Rodin. I guess money talks... Maybe he showed up right when they had no other option but to accept it. My parents seemed like the type to get into debt.

Oh, Rodin's still waiting for me to answer his question.

"I—used my magic...on fairies. Didn't know to...give it...to the spider...originally."

The first time I saw one of my family's spiders, I screamed. I was only a baby, and this huge, scary spider had come up to me and put its front legs (is that what they're called?) on my head! It was my father's spider.

I started bawling in confusion, and a maid clamped her hand over my mouth and nose until I almost suffocated.

At the time, I didn't yet understand the native language, but my father had probably told the maid something along the lines of "Make her shut up!" Sure, the maid was about to kill me without a second thought, but my father observed her doing that with delight. That's when I realized that he was as bad as my father from my previous life.

I was glad that my spider was actually adorable, as opposed to my father's. I sensed that unlike the rest of the Nuir household, my little spider was on my side.

Urgh... I've been talking a lot more than usual. My jaw hurts, and my throat's parched.

I took a sip of tea, not minding that a fairy had snuck in and was treating it like a hot tub. Fairies were always getting into my food and drink, so it was nothing unusual for me, but Argit, who could see them, seemed a bit startled.

Don't worry. I'm not gonna eat it.

The fairy was pretending to cling to the teacup rim, having a grand old time.

They didn't indicate that they were in any trouble, so I continued where I left off.

"Later...I learned about spiders... But by then I—I didn't want to...use my power for...my family." Toward the end, my voice became very hoarse and quiet.

"I see... You should rest now. The blessweaving might not have exhausted you, but speaking seems to," said Argit, seemingly amazed by what he had heard from me. I nodded.

"You said she can also heal fairies?" he asked Skur.

"Indeed. She can control how and when to use magic like a sorceress."

Hmm? Does Argit want to see me heal a fairy? But none of the fairies here need any healing...

I spun a thread of magic, and with a practiced hand...or I guess, a practiced mind (?)...fashioned a lacy cape for a nearby fairy.

Sure, Argit could see what I was doing...not that I minded. I'd gotten so used to mending fairies' clothes that it was practically second nature. Plus, I didn't yet have an inkling about how incredible my magic thread was.

"You are a phenomenon, Yui," said Argit. "Not only can you make thread out of magic, but you also seem to be able to freely manipulate it as you see fit."

"She can shape her magic into a needle and spin someone else's magic into a thread to work with, too," Skur added.

"Did I hear that right?"

"Other people's magic must be more difficult for her to control, hence the needle to guide it. Rather than make the threads move with her willpower, she holds the needle and sews as if using ordinary materials. This is how she healed these fairies. They helped her make threads out of my magic."

Skur showed Argit the kitty-eared fairies.

"Incredible."

"Buh?"

"It normally takes a very long time for fairies to grow accustomed to a human by slowly absorbing some of their magic and making it their own. They then may become that person's familiars. I'd never heard of anyone who could take another's magic and transfer it to the fairies in this way."

"I can't...force it...on them."

"You do it at their request?"

I nodded firmly.

"You see what I'm saying," commented Skur, eliciting a lopsided smile from Argit.

"That's certainly more efficient than waiting until the fairies naturally absorb the magic trickling out of people. I see you've been hard at work in this household."

I have. And now pretty much everyone in this household has their own fairy companions.

◆

After taking a break in Argit's lap, I picked up my needle again.

Seeing I was ready to resume sewing more clothes for Argit, Rodin told me to use as much of the fabric provided by Skur and Ulde as I needed. My eyes lit up with excitement.

"But I do ask you not to overwork yourself. Tell me at once when you start feeling tired."

I gathered that Rodin was curious to see what my limits were when it came to blessweaving.

I bet the shoddy blessweaving in Argit's clothing proves the limited amount of magic power at the Nuirs' disposal. They only made blessed clothes for the king, after all. And if Argit's outfit is any indication, they really suck at it!

I quickly threw together a few sets of casual shirts, pants, and underwear for Argit. Maybe I'd leveled up (?) along the way, since I was now definitely stitching faster than a sewing machine. Next, I was going to make him a military uniform, two suits (one like a mafia boss, and the other host club–inspired), a regular coat, and a fur coat, too.

Aw, I don't have enough fur for that. Okay—maybe some fur accents, at least? Or a fur collar!

Lastly, I was going to make him some clothes typically worn by high-ranking nobility.

This would be so much easier if zippers existed...or even rubber bands.

Maybe I could get someone to make me snap fasteners if I explained what they should look like? Ooh, and belt buckles, too...

I was lost in my thoughts, so I didn't notice when the fairies gathered around the superfluous gems I'd pruned from Argit's original outfit. They were opening their mouths as if asking to be fed.

"Buh?"

"They want to lend you their power. They must have sensed you had a wish. Try offering them some magic," Argit advised.

I sent out magic threads toward the open-mouthed fairies, and they chomped down on the ends. It looked like I'd plugged them into an outlet.

The fairies gathered some of the gems...mixed them, stretched them out...

Just as I thought they might be making a belt buckle, the fairies paused and looked at me questioningly.

"While your magic connects you to the fairies, you can communicate what you want in detail."

"Myuh..."

I'd never seen fairies transform real objects, and here they were combining the gems like sugar candy, stretching them out and folding them in. I was fascinated.

I wonder if they can separate the gems by color and distribute them? Green for the leaves and vines, red for the berries. Something with a mix of gold and silver. And something with a more muted palette.

The next thing I knew, the fairies had made an assortment of belt buckles for me.

Amazing!

I panicked for a moment when I realized I didn't have any leather to make belts, so I resorted to using thick, sturdy fabric instead. The fairies punched holes in the belts for me, then I altered a few pairs of pants, and voilà—done!

Hmm, I'm having too much fun with this. Too flashy, maybe? But he'd look so good in these! He has enough natural elegance to make up for his original trashy getup.

I'll have to ask the fairies to make some chic accessories for him, too, to go with the military uniform and suits. Shame I don't know how zippers are made.

"Are you satisfied with the result?" Argit asked me with a strange smile playing on his lips, picking up one belt after another to examine them.

"?"

"You've witnessed real fairy magic at work. It's not like sorcery, where a magician is in control of what happens—you supplied the fairies with your magic, and they used it how they saw fit. It's extremely rare for fairies to do such a favor for those with faysight, or magicians."

I had my magic threads, so I wasn't that surprised that the fairies, or my spider, had magic of their own.

Magic! Sorcery!

Fairies seemed to be entwined with both. What was the difference between fairy magic and regular (?) magic, though? And why hadn't anything like this happened before, when I was experimenting with my magic threads soon after learning how to use them? I bet there's some sort of fairy affinity involved. Or going back to what Argit said about communicating with them in detail, was it because I didn't make my wishes clear enough? So much of how this world worked remained a complete mystery to me.

"I think Yui has done enough for one day." Concerned about me overworking myself, Ulde snatched me up into her arms. "Yui's sewing is

certainly a wonder to behold, but Linne told me that she tends to become so engrossed in her work that she forgoes eating and sleeping. She's been scheduled to work only until noon and spend afternoons convalescing."

"?!"

Nooo! I was in the middle of making the host-club suit!

"Oh, lunch already?" Rodin checked the clock. "I was so entranced by Yui's craft, I hadn't noticed how much time had passed."

"Nwah?"

While my attention was focused on Ulde and Rodin, Argit had changed out of the yukata and into the black military uniform.

Wow—he looks even cooler than I'd pictured! Now I'm getting really into this!

But wait...

"How is...the fit?" I asked.

I'm a seamstress, first and foremost. Unfortunately, that was the moment my throat decided to tighten up, and I erupted in a coughing fit. My jaw was still hurting, too. A clear sign that was enough talking for one day.

Ulde rubbed my back, and Argit brought a cup to my mouth. I took a grateful sip—it was hot water with honey (that a fairy had soaked in), and it was delicious. It didn't help with my jaw pain, maybe because fairy energy didn't work on aching muscles, but it did alleviate my sore throat. Maybe the inflammation was from all the talking? The doctor had warned me not to raise my voice too much or I might cough up blood.

I still tired very quickly. Everyone urged me to take frequent breaks, and I knew I should heed their advice. Also, as soon as I snapped out of my hyperfocus on sewing, my body felt heavy and sluggish. I used to go without eating or drinking for long periods of time back at the Nuir residence. Ironically, it felt as if I'd become weaker since coming here, as after my body recovered from its emaciated state, it demanded to be treated with more care. It'd probably take a bit longer for my stamina to catch up to my physical development.

"The fit couldn't be more perfect." Argit smiled and stroked my hair. "You're amazing, Yui."

"?"

"Are you aware of how valued blessweaving is in our kingdom?"

I was about to reply, but he put his finger to my lips to stop me.

"I apologize. I shouldn't ask you to speak any more today."

It was just a rhetorical question anyway. He knew how ignorant I was—he'd seen me try to cut his enchanted clothes with scissors.

I used to have only a vague idea of what blessweaving did—that it imbued fabric with fairy energy or something. I didn't expect it to have particularly tangible effects, such as repelling blades. If anything, it was just part of the Nuirs' work...

"I'll tell you about it in detail later, but for now, you must know two things. Firstly, that your blessweaving is particularly good. And secondly, that this carries a significant danger."

Huh? What danger?

I cocked my head questioningly, to which Argit responded by taking my right hand and planting a kiss on my index finger.

Whoaaa! It's like I'm in a movie!

"I, Argit Lomestometlo, hereby ask you—Yui, Maiden of the Needle—for your hand in marriage."

"Myuh?"
M-marriage?!

"Yui, I'll explain everything later. For now, you'll keep your name," Rodin quickly added.

Before I did anything, I paused to think this over.

Argit didn't look like a creep to me. He treated me just like a child. So then why did he want to marry me? Was it to protect me? Apparently, bless-weaving was a lot more valuable than I thought. Plus, my looks made me a magnet for pervs who were into little girls. I also possessed faysight, which qualified me to become a lover (or spouse?) of a royal. So maybe I had a target on my back for social climbers?

My father's ugly face flashed in my mind, and I went pale.

"Yui, are you all right? You don't look well."

"Go back...to...the Nuirs?" I asked, briefly forgetting about my aching jaw.

Argit and Rodin must have realized where I was headed with this, because they looked a bit exasperated.

"You figured it out."

"What you just said, Yui—that's precisely what we're trying to avoid."

I hurriedly took Argit's hand and kissed his index finger like he did mine.

"I, Yui...agree to...marry you."

The dining room they took me to after that wasn't the one for the servants where I'd been eating until then. A magnificent dining table with six chairs was in the middle of the room. This must have been where Rodin ate when entertaining high-ranking guests. But what was I doing there?

He noticed my confused expression.

"Since you're now engaged to His Highness, your social standing is higher than mine. Should I call you Lady Yui from now on?"

I shook my head furiously.

Come to think of it, I *was* an aristocrat. The Nuirs had hired tutors to teach me the basics of etiquette, reading and writing, and some general information about the world. Except my learning was stop-start, since no sooner had a tutor been hired than they'd be dismissed—because they would notify my parents about the servants' cruel treatment toward me. But my parents weren't the sort of people to care about my well-being, so rather than warn or fire the servants, it was the tutors they'd let go. They didn't want people with a conscience in their house. I'd warned the last of my tutors about this, so she stayed the longest, but in the end, she too was dismissed.

I didn't feel like a noble, to be honest. Just a common seamstress. That was probably because I still retained memories of my past life, plus the past five years of being treated like a slave by my own family.

Rodin and Argit noticed how perplexed I was by my sudden change of status in the household, and they chuckled.

"Don't be so alarmed, Yui," Argit urged. "Consider Rodin your guardian. A fatherly presence... No, he's too young for that. A *brotherly* presence in your life."

"When I hired you to work for me, your parents renounced their guardianship of you, as per our contract," said Rodin.

I fixated on the word *renounced*. What a huge relief!

"Your pact with your spider, though—that's a problem we've yet to solve." Argit's voice was thoughtful, serious.

I craned my neck to look at my spider, which was sitting on my shoulder, playing with my hair. It was the size of my palm...so like me, it had grown.

Back at the Nuir residence, it'd remained motionless most of the time. Ever since I moved to Rodin's home and my health improved, my spider had become more active. When I cocked my head, it mimicked me; other times, it would hide in and play with my hair. Maybe it'd been conserving energy like my emaciated body had.

"I wouldn't put it past your father not to ensure your spider caused no harm... I haven't seen the pact, and I suspect neither did you?" Rodin asked.

Was there some problem with my spider?

"Have they taught you that the Nuirs' spiders were originally monsters that preyed on fairies and caused all sorts of harm in the world?"

I nodded. When I was bedridden, the maids brought me an illustrated book about the origins of the kingdom. That's where I read about the spiders, too.

◆

A long time ago, there was a young maiden pure of heart who could see fairies. One day, she came across a very peculiar monster. It was a monstrous spider—creatures known to devour fairies—surrounded by fairies who seemed rather fond of it. The maiden cautiously approached the beast and found it to be gentle and wise, with an aura of holiness. The spider taught her many things, the art of sewing among them. The girl and the spider became friends.

She grew up into a smart, beautiful woman, and many men tried to win her heart. The spider could see through them, and it kept the greedy ones and the fools at bay. The fools and the greedy ones hired mercenaries to kill the spider, thinking that once it was gone, they would easily make the woman theirs. But the mercenaries were avaricious, too, and they desired the beautiful woman for themselves. They plotted to kill the spider, take the money, and then abduct the woman. Yet they were no match for the spider, who was both wise and powerful.

Then one day, an evil magician who hurt fairies to steal their power kidnapped the fairies who were friends with the woman and the spider, then held them hostage. The kindhearted girl and spider could not fight the mercenaries back, lest the magician kill their fairy friends. Thus, the spider did not try to defend itself when a mercenary swung his sword at it. The woman leaped in between the blade and the spider in order to save it. But before the sword struck her, a young man—who also could see the fairies and was quick-witted and good-natured—deflected the blade.

This man was to become the founder of the kingdom, the first king of House Lomestometlo, and the young woman was to become his wife and the first queen.

◆

That was, in a nutshell, the first part of the story I read in that book.

"What actually happened was that the lady who was to found House Nuir had been abducted and thrown into a labyrinth infested with bloodthirsty monsters. It was her father who rescued her from it. That's why the pact with the spiders is only valid for those of Nuir blood, not of Lomestometlo."

"Was it her older brother who took the crown? Or maybe it was the younger one; the sources are not clear on that."

"The spider that protected her from the monsters in the labyrinth was a divine beast."

Divine beasts.

Argit explained that these extremely uncommon creatures possessed powerful magic and great wisdom.

"Very, very rarely, a monster may transform into a divine beast. Their offspring are clones, but clones of their original monster form. The head of the Nuir family controls their reproduction through a pact with the spiders in order to stop aggressive monster spiders from proliferating."

No surprise there. Although, thinking about my father being in charge of all this made me anxious.

Argit went into further detail. Unlike monsters, divine beasts didn't harm fairies. They were sentient and able to use magic. Their offspring had a fair chance to hatch as divine beasts, so they were looked after with great care. But since spiders were originally monsters, they were difficult to control.

"It's necessary for the head of your family to change your pact with the spiders when you marry, or it will become invalid when your family name changes," Argit explained. "Your spider would no longer be subject to its restrictions."

Rodin frowned; this worrying information, apparently new to him, seemed to be giving him a headache. Argit offered a strained smile and carried on.

"That's why we'll first need you to become the head of your household, Yui."

If I'd started eating my soup just then, I would've spat it out all over the table. That's how shocked I was. I'd been living in my happy little bubble as nothing more than a seamstress, and now that bubble had burst.

I must've pulled a strange face. The maids setting the table paused for a moment and looked at me with concern.

"The spiders' pact with the head of the Nuir family contains a definition of head of the family, which is the member of the family with the highest level of skill. Which would already qualify you, and to make it official, we just need the approval of King Amnart," Argit said nonchalantly, eating his meal with effortless elegance. "Things would have been so much different had Yui's uncle become the head of the Nuirs instead of her father."

"I've heard rumors that her father and grandfather murdered him…"

That was the first I'd ever heard of my father having a brother. Given how nasty the man was, I could see how he'd rather kill his older brother than make an effort to surpass him. He and my grandfather must have been cut from the same cloth. Maybe the two got along because they were equally rotten.

"I don't want to live the rest of my life regretting not having stepped in to take the vulnerable Nuir under my wing, like my father did," said Rodin.

What I was hearing was truly horrific, but I didn't feel in danger. Rodin was trustworthy and capable, as corroborated by his servants.

"Yui, you should eat."

At Rodin's insistence, I picked up my spoon and tried the soup. It was as delicious as always, and it made me realize that I was in fact very hungry. My jaw was aching, though, and I'd rather avoid having to eat anything that required chewing. Would it be crass if I dunked my slice of bread in the soup?

Hmm, better not do that.

I tore off a small piece, put it in my mouth, and quickly followed up with a spoonful of soup to soften it.

"Your engagement to me will offer you protection," Argit explained. "It will help keep you out of power struggles at the palace as well. As the former king, I don't have any official powers, but I still wield considerable influence."

"You'd probably be happy living as a simple seamstress, Yui, but knowing of your talents, it would have been cruel of me to keep you all to myself while the royalty of our kingdom had to dress in pathetic clothes like you've seen," Rodin said, taking out the scented sachet I'd made him as a gift.

Ohhh, so that's *how he realized I can blessweave!*

I didn't regret making the sachets, though—I'd taken into consideration that my secret might be discovered.

"Your children won't inherit the right to the crown after you marry me," said Argit. "I don't mind if you were to have children with someone else, a person of your choosing."

Whuh? What in the world is he talking about?

He reached out to me and stroked my cheek with his big hand.

"It's bad for digestion not to chew your food properly. Oh... Is it because your jaw hurts?"

Aha, he noticed.

"Well, most days, she'll say only a few words at best. Oftentimes, she just replies with catlike noises," Rodin told him.

"Catlike noises?"

They didn't strain me as much as talking and were a good way to convey emotion when I couldn't remember the right words to use. Granted, maybe I'd been resorting to them more than necessary, out of habit. Considering my looks, it wasn't all that out of character.

The servants took away my food and brought me something pureed, like what you'd give to a baby. By the time I finished it, I was irresistibly sleepy.

"It's not from magic exhaustion, is it?"

"No, she's just physically exhausted."

I heard their voices, but they sounded so far away.

*   *   *

Wait... I'm not finished...sewing...

◆

Yui passed out with her head on the dining table. Argit smiled lopsidedly, gazing at her. She looked sweet and delicate, as if she were a confectioner's masterpiece made of sugar. Yet she also possessed a bewitching aura, as if she weren't quite of this world.

He'd only had the chance to observe her for a brief time, but he could already see that her personality was very much unlike her appearance. She also didn't long for romance like other girls her age.

She was also exceptionally vulnerable. He understood why Rodin had approached him about her with such urgency.

Yui's talent for blessweaving matched the most illustrious of her ancestors. The fairies loved her and willingly bestowed their blessings on her. She even looked like a fairy with her otherworldly beauty.

She looked very young for her age, but despite that... No, *because* of that, she might be targeted by influential men with twisted intentions.

Rodin had likely arrived at the conclusion that only a person with the highest authority, who was at the same time unfettered by political commitments, would be able to protect this purehearted, gifted seamstress. When he'd disclosed to Argit what he wanted his help with, Argit had assumed at first that the girl was in love with Rodin. That was how it usually went, didn't it? A girl saved from abuse would fall for her savior, especially when he was as handsome as Rodin. But Yui only had love for one thing.

"She's a strange kind of prodigy, isn't she? Her sole concern is whether she'll be able to carry on with her needlework."

"This single-mindedness might be what enabled her to achieve the highest level of craftsmanship at such a young age."

Yui was an artisan entirely devoted to her craft. Argit couldn't be more pleased.

◆

The first wife of the former king, Argit Lomestometlo, wasn't the kind of person who left a strong impression.

When Argit ascended the throne at age twelve, he chose to marry a fay-sighted girl who was two years older than him and therefore of childbearing age. She'd always call for her nanny and had her manage every aspect of her life. Argit couldn't remember ever having anything that amounted to a conversation with his first wife.

The nanny in question was a domineering old lady who shamelessly pestered everyone around to shower the young queen with expensive gifts and cater to her every whim, even at their own expense. Argit felt sorry, in a way, for his first wife, who'd been raised by this unpleasant person.

They conceived Amnart, the next king-to-be, on the night of the consummation of their marriage. Giving birth to him was likely his first wife's greatest achievement—that, and her death soon after.

Argit made sure that the late queen's nanny would have no hand in raising their baby. Instead, he had his most trusted people look after him. The nanny objected; she wanted to influence Amnart, and her obsession with him was most unsightly. Argit had to ensure that his son was carefully guarded at all times.

The queen was just a pitiable marionette, ruled by her nanny, without any interest in anything in life. Even her baby son's natural love for his mother was quashed after a single interaction with her.

Argit had only married her out of lack of other suitable candidates. But perhaps that was for the best. Had he married someone else, the vicious, fanatical nanny might have attempted to harm her charge out of spite.

The next woman he married came from a neighboring country, where she'd been persecuted for her faysight, which was a largely unknown ability in her homeland.

At first, she, too, hardly spoke. Her eyes were vacant as if she were dead inside. Her country was keen to be rid of her, and so she was forced to marry Argit.

Faysight was extremely rare in her homeland, and those who possessed that gift were unfortunately singled out as aberrant and discriminated against.

She fell in love with Argit after marrying him, but tragically, this love morphed into unhealthy dependence. She became morbidly jealous of any women Argit came in contact with, losing grip on reality. She even envied his first wife and the fairies. By the time Argit noticed just how bad her mental state had gotten, she'd become a faymancer, causing harm to fairies, and she'd even injured the Realm Weaveguardian.

Consequently, she was convicted of treason. Argit divorced her, and she was banished from the kingdom. He took responsibility for what had happened by stepping down from the throne.

He had repeatedly cautioned his wife that he disapproved of people who hurt and took advantage of others for their own gain, yet the lovestruck woman failed to heed his warnings.

◆

Argit had never fallen in love with anyone. His two wives had only caused him frustration. The young girl he offered to marry this time had as pitiful a background as previous spouses, yet he was smitten...by her love for her craft.

Thinking back, he'd always had more respect for girls and women who pursued their passions in life rather than men.

"She's one of a kind."

"It seems she's sound asleep... Have you brought with you her new personal maid, Your Highness? I would like her to come along to speak with the doctor who's been looking after Yui, so that he may brief her about Yui's health and the next steps for her recovery as well as any accommodations that should be made for her."

"Oh..." Argit looked at the ceiling. "I did bring someone, but now I'm not sure whether it was the right choice."

Argit picked up the sleeping Yui in his arms and carried her to the servants' waiting room...where a maid had been lying sprawled over the sofa in a most inelegant manner. She jumped to her feet and stood at attention.

"Welcome back, Master..."

While she looked to be the same age as Yui, she was actually in her midtwenties. She was a northerner of mixed race, with some Terra ancestors. Her black hair was tied in pigtails, which made her look deceptively like a little girl—a fact she liked to play to her advantage.

Yui's new maid-to-be, for all appearances a complete novice, boldly walked up to Argit.

"Oh-ho-ho! She's a cutie!" She ogled the girl, waving her arms like an excited creeper. "I can't believe she's from that rotten House Nuir! The only traits she must have inherited must have come from her most distant ancestors!" The maid cleared her throat loudly and pursed her lips, which was ill-suited to her charming looks. "A true sleeping beauty... Should I wake her up with a kiss?"

"Hands off, you perv!"

"Bwah!"

A woman clad in full-body armor stepped out of the shadows and smacked the pervy maid on the head with her sheathed sword, sending her flying. The maid hit a wall and fell silent. This kind of impact might kill a person, yet neither Argit nor the armored woman seemed fazed at all.

"My apologies, Stolle. I didn't know Yui was the type she's obsessed with... I'm afraid you'll have your work cut out for you."

"I'm used to her being a handful."

The top-class royal maid Argit had brought with him was not only trained as a housekeeper, but also as an assassin and warrior. She had an extensive network of informants and could even use sorcery. Her only weakness was her fanatical love of beautiful young girls. She was a pervert through and through, so much so that she'd swoon even over her own reflection in the mirror.

"You talk like you're better than me, Stolle, but I bet that in your heart you were screaming with delight, your fantasies about having a beautiful princess to protect finally come true," said Mimachi, who'd peeled herself off the wall.

"Not everyone thinks like you, pervert."

"Stolle!"

Rodin, who'd been too shocked to know how to react earlier, brightened up and walked over to the knight, Stolle, whose air of disciplined dignity gave way to sudden bashfulness.

"R-Rodin... It's good to see you."

Rodin planted a kiss on her gauntlet-protected hand.

"It's been so long. An entire week." He smiled at her dazzlingly, with great fondness.

"Seven days isn't long at all," Mimachi, the maid, butted in, oblivious to the romantic tension between Rodin and the knight completely concealed by her (feminine but nevertheless) armor.

"Oh? I thought you knew, Mimachi—that Rodin and Stolle are lovers," Argit explained matter-of-factly to Mimachi, who'd recovered from the wall-slam damage. (She'd healed up from the scabbard hit almost immediately.)

"Ohhh-ho-hooo! You're not joking, are you?! I thought the defenses around her heart were as impregnable as her armor, and you're telling me she's lovers with the dreamy Rodin Calostira, the most desired young man who sends shivers down the spines of all maidens of marriageable age?"

"Stop with your annoying blather, pervert!"

"Moving on—this is Yui. I have given her the title of the Maiden of the Needle," Argit announced, sitting down in a chair while still holding Yui bridal style.

It was customary to give one's betrothed a special title—a nickname—upon engagement. Among nobility, an engagement might be canceled outright should the suitor be unable to think of an appropriate title.

"You are now engaged, Your Highness?"

"Oh-ho-ho! A tender, young wife—isn't that every man's dream?! Great choice, Master! You're still sprightly and good-looking for a middle-aged man! You're looking even more handsome now, somehow!"

"Yui turned out to be far more talented than I'd expected, based on the scented sachets she made."

Only then did Mimachi and Stolle notice his new clothes. They both gasped.

"Your magical power has shot up!"

"She really is as gifted as the Founder. Your Highness, you haven't changed your mind about assigning me and Mimachi to her, have you? Are you still certain that Mimachi is a good choice for the role? It's Mimachi, after all."

"You're being mean, Stolle!"

"Hmm, well. I think you will do fine."

Mimachi was a bit of a creep and a loudmouth, but she could do the work of ten maids on her own easily, and she would also serve as a bodyguard. Argit had no better option for ensuring Yui's safety.

"...I hereby ask you to serve my betrothed. Be her support. Be her protection."

The maid and the knight stood at attention, each putting her right hand on her left breast.

"I pledge to support her."

"And I pledge to protect her."

94

CHAPTER 5

Flower~Crowned Armor

When I woke up, I was introduced to two young women. The first was Mimachi, my new personal maid, a girl with some Terra ancestry. She was almost Lolita-esque and looked very cute, although in a different way from me. I was told that despite her youthful appearance, she was a grown woman. Her black hair done up in pigtails was very Japanese, in a way.

She had the same vibe as one of my friends from my past life who often asked me to make her costumes based on anime or video game characters. This friend was so into her cosplay that she even worked out to sculpt her tummy into a six-pack. She actually paid me for those costumes, too, although I had no idea where she got all that money from. She could overcome any difficulty to keep doing what she loved. Honestly, if it weren't for her, I don't know if I'd have found the strength to stand up to my family. The resemblance is why I instantly gravitated toward Mimachi.

The other woman was a knight assigned as my personal guard. Her name was Stolle Menes, and apparently, she was Rodin's girlfriend. Her family kept the peace in the lands where Argit had dwelled since retirement. I couldn't tell what she looked like, since she was covered in armor from head to toe. I wasn't paying that much attention to what Argit was telling me about her, though, because...

...something was *very* wrong with her!

"Please...take off...your armor... *Cough!*"

"E-excuse me? Lady Yui...?"

I never expected to see another person dressed as outrageously badly as Argit. Why was Stolle wearing something so stumpy? It completely defeated the purpose of ladies' armor. She looked more like a samurai than a woman, for crying out loud!

"Um, you see, Lady Yui...women from Stolle's family are forbidden from taking their armor off in front of a man until they get married," Mimachi explained, stroking my back.

"Are you and Rodin...?" Stolle asked me quietly in a quivering voice.

I shook my head back and forth. They'd mistakenly assumed I had a crush on Rodin and was jealous of Stolle, but of course, I didn't feel that way at all. Rodin never had romantic intentions toward me, and neither did I to him—he was my guardian, the man who'd rescued me, a nearly starved, neglected child.

"Wearing...wrong..." was all I managed to say before completely losing my voice. My throat hurt less after resting earlier, but I was still very worn out from all the talking.

Mimachi held out her hands to me.

"Don't strain your voice, Lady Yui," she urged. "Just mouth what you want to say, okay? I'll read your lips."

Oh! Lipreading!

My problem wasn't just that I couldn't physically speak, but that I had

trouble remembering the right words. I still tried my best to communicate, even though I couldn't use full sentences.

I'd spoken the local language perfectly up until I was ten years old, but after five years of hardly talking at all, it'd gotten mixed up in my head with Japanese.

"Um, she's saying the neck part should be at the bottom? And then something about the legs?" said Mimachi, interpreting for me. "The breast protector... Tighten it like a corset?"

"With all due respect, Lady Yui, armor is not worn like a corset."

I shook my head.

"I—I cannot fight in a corset!" Stolle insisted.

"Hmm... You can't, um, tighten the chest piece somehow?"

"Women's breasts are soft and require proper protection! Protecting weak spots is the whole point of wearing armor!"

"And you've got a lot of volume to protect there, huh, Stolle?"

Stolle grabbed Mimachi's face, digging her gauntlet's iron claws into the maid's skin.

"You're not actually interpreting what Lady Yui is saying, are you, you lecher?!"

"D-don't pick me uuup!"

Stolle's full-body armor seemed to be a mix of both male and female armor pieces. Armor was outside my field of expertise, but even I could see what was wrong with it.

She was wearing a scale-armor cuirass with a blesswoven skirt. It wasn't made by my father, at least not alone. Maybe he'd collaborated with an armorsmith on it. I could sense magic in the metal parts, but if the armor wasn't worn correctly, the magic wasn't linking up properly, either. Which was even more of a shame, seeing as the armor was quite well-made.

Stolle couldn't remove her armor in front of men, but it shouldn't be a problem if it was just in front of me and Mimachi.

I glanced at Argit and Rodin. They smiled awkwardly and nodded in understanding.

"Lady Yui reacted similarly when she saw His Highness for the first time," said Rodin. "The armor Stolle is wearing, though, is a prized Menes family heirloom."

"Don't take it apart," Argit whispered in my ear.

I nodded. "It's...not used right..."

Once Argit, Rodin, and the doctor left the room, several maids entered.

Hold on. This is the doctor's office? What am I doing here? The last thing I remember is falling asleep in the dining room...

"Well, Stolle, let me help you get undressed!" said Mimachi.

"What? Huh?"

"Hweh-hweh-hweh! Come on! Off with the armor!"

Mimachi flapped her arms excitedly, ready to pounce on Stolle...but before she had the chance to do that, Rodin's housekeeper appeared out of nowhere and grabbed her by the neck from behind. She lifted the lecherous maid into the air with just one hand.

Wait... Huh? This lady is crazy strong... Doesn't that count as strangling? Is Mimachi okay?

"And so we meet again, Mimachi."

"What a...ugh...pleasure, Lady Endelia..."

"I heard you've been chosen to be Lady Yui's personal maid. You will come with me now so that I can pass on important instructions to you."

"I-I'd love to talk to you, but I'm afraid I cannot leave my mistress's side," Mimachi replied. She shot me a pleading, terrified look; a stiff smile was plastered on her pale face, and her knees were shaking.

"Lady Yui, may I borrow her for a moment?" Endelia asked me.

"Yes."

I agreed without hesitation. Of course I didn't mind. The other maids didn't even shoot us curious looks, knowing full well that Endelia's requests were never denied.

"Lady Yui?! You can't be serious!" Mimachi wailed.

After Mimachi's forceful removal, the maids set about helping Stolle take off her armor. Someone had left me writing paper and a quill on a nearby table. The maids had anticipated my every need. I drew a simple illustration of how the armor should be worn and handed it back to the maids. Once they examined it, they began laying out the pieces of armor in the order they should be put on.

Meanwhile, I was given a viscous drink that looked like syrup.

"?"

I didn't really want to be distracted from my work even for a moment, but the maids stared daggers at me, urging me to drink the beverage.

"You mustn't be so careless of your health, Lady Yui. Especially now that you're engaged to His Highness!"

"No one's saying you should give up needlework. Just take better care of yourself."

Relief washed over me. There was a worry in the corner of my mind that I might be forced to stop working if I married such an important person, and it must have shown. I calmed down when one of the maids patted my head...although being called "Lady" by everyone felt a little awkward.

The maids finished laying out the armor in the correct order. Stolle had been standing, waiting, exposed. She had creamy skin, and her long hair, with which she modestly covered her breasts, was a buttery blond. It returned to its natural shape immediately after she removed her helmet, so it must have been strong and healthy.

Her eyes were blue, and since her skin tone was so light, their vibrant color was even more striking. She wasn't just cute—she was a real beauty. Quiet, gentle, and very serious, she would make the perfect librarian.

I thought it was adorable how different she appeared with and without her armor on. And to think that Rodin had never seen what she looked like! He was a remarkable man, falling in love with Stolle based on her personality alone. I figured he would become even crazier about her once he discovered what she was like underneath that armor.

As for her body shape... She was very sizable up top, with a narrow waist and curvy hips. I couldn't guess her measurements when she had her armor on, so I took a good look at her...

...

......

....

I was staring so intently, my brow creased from effort. I had mentioned before that they did have underwear of sorts in this world. Except that from my point of view, it was not fit for its purpose. So many women were binding their breasts or wearing tight corsets—or, in Stolle's case, a suit of armor! It was a miracle she could move around in it.

"The brassiere...needs to be...one size bigger... *Cough!*"

The maids' eyes lit up mischievously.

"Is that so, Lady Yui?!"

I nodded and wrote down the size on a piece of paper I'd been given. Stolle was about the same size as the housekeeper, Endelia, so there should have been some spares in the storeroom.

"What? Wait—I'm perfectly fine with what I'm wearing now!"

"It only seems so to you at the moment, Lady Stolle! All of us have followed Lady Yui's advice and went up by one or even two sizes. Without the

proper support, all that volume simply gets pushed elsewhere! To your stomach, or to your back!"

Putting on a corset was a real hassle, so most people didn't wear them correctly. I had one maid demonstrate the difference a well-fitted bra could make, and they all agreed it was far better. Once the breasts were contained rather than flattened, a woman could fill a bra one or two sizes bigger than what she was used to... A frightening experience indeed.

The maids tore their saddened gazes away from Stolle.

"A-are you sure I need a bigger size?" Stolle asked hesitantly, covering her breasts with her hands.

I nodded at her, recognizing the fear in her eyes. I'd experienced it as well in my past life. She'd been squishing her breasts too much this entire time. I hadn't noticed that outright because of her armor.

"Lady Yui only needs to take one look at a lady's chest to know her size. Her *true* size!"

"Some women prefer to bind their breasts tight to get them out of the way, but believe me, if you wear a bra like Lady Yui shows you, you'll find it to be both more comfortable and practical!"

"B-by the way, I couldn't help noticing that you all seem more radiant and beautiful than the last time I saw you..."

"Ah, that's because some of the fairies' blessings for Lady Yui trickle down to us, too!"

They seemed to think it was only a temporary effect. I quickly put up my hand, thinking I should clarify that misunderstanding.

"You have...your own— *Cough!*"

"Lady Yui, please, you shouldn't talk! I'll get you another piece of paper—just a moment!"

One maid brought me more paper to write on.

I'd only found out earlier that day that everyone in Rodin's household now had their own fairy familiar. When I healed the fairies Skur had brought, the other fairies present saw how I could use another person's magic to mend their clothes. After that, they went around looking for people whose magic was to their liking. They then spun it into threads for me to use on them.

Most people weren't even aware of their own magic, which rose from their bodies like a faint haze. They weren't able to control how much magic they were letting out, either. The fairies would normally absorb this magic a little bit at a time from the people they liked so that they could eventually become their familiars. But I could make this process far quicker by sewing the magic into the fairies' clothes.

Endelia already had companion fairies, so I didn't do anything special for her. But whenever I saw fairies hovering around someone with magic threads ready, I did my best to beautify their garments...not suspecting for a moment that by doing that, I was turning them into those people's familiars.

I wrote down on the piece of paper that everyone in the house now had their guardian fairies.

"Oh my."

"No way! Ah, but actually, I did notice that my tea tastes better even without Lady Yui nearby..."

"Yes, now that I think of it, I noticed things like that, too..."

"This information could be dangerous... It's fortunate that His Highness Argit is visiting today. It goes without saying that—"

"Not a word about this to anyone from outside the household, of course."

"Except His Highness. I will go and speak of this with Master Rodin later."

"Lady Yui! Everything is ready for Lady Stolle!"

Stolle shrieked as I tugged and pulled to stuff her breasts into the bra properly.

Putting a bra on by yourself and having someone else do it for you were two very different things. Someone had done this to me once as well—an older girl in the school crafts club I'd been a member of. I spaced out a little, remembering that incident.

That's when I went up two cup sizes...

In my past life, my mother was basically a glorified housekeeper, so she didn't dress fashionably. She didn't teach me anything, really, not just about how to dress but in general. She relied on my father's judgment in every aspect of life, having no will or initiative of her own. It never occurred to her to show me how to wear a bra properly or do anything for my appearance. I learned all those things from my friends and classmates instead.

One thing an upperclassman told me especially stuck in my mind— that life is a battle, and the clothes a woman wears are her armor.

I picked up the quill and paper and noted down more detailed instructions and hints for putting on Stolle's armor. Although she seemed confused, Stolle got dressed following my step-by-step guide.

"I can't believe it! I don't need to tie the strings of the cuirass any tighter—it all fits just right!"

The armor now fitted her silhouette, and she seemed quite pleased with the result. But something else was about to change:

The hornlike protrusion on her helmet began twisting.

"Whaaat...?"

A murmur swept through the room. Everyone was surprised, myself included! What initially looked to be a horn had twisted around the helmet and sprouted blooming flowers.

"It's so pretty..."

"Incredible!"

The maids gasped in wonder. Stolle's helmet now featured a crown of lilies.

Next, green gems emerged from the cuirass, sliding up to arrange themselves over Stolle's collarbones.

And then a fairy emerged from the breastplate and stretched out their wings. (Nobody could see them but me.)

I'd never seen a fairy this big before. They were as tall as the suit of armor. They must have been lying dormant, concealed in the breastplate. After a big stretch and shaking out their limbs, the fairy fused with the armor again, and I could no longer see them.

I'd just witnessed something extraordinary, a type of fairy I'd never encountered before—an armor fairy. They were an artificial fairy born from the armor. This had to be blessweaving at the very highest level of mastery.

It could create new fairies!

"This is fantastic! My armor feels as light as a feather! Even I feel lighter somehow!"

Stolle was noticing the effects but hadn't yet seen how her armor had transformed. She was waving her arms excitedly.

"It doesn't feel hot at all, either! And it's easier to breathe, even more so than without the armor! The air smells nicer, too, somehow!"

Of course everything was better—she was *wearing* a fairy. It had to be even more beneficial than eating food or drinking beverages touched by fairies or bathing together with them. Ordinary fairies sometimes came into contact with humans and animals when hiding among plants or in the soil, but they wouldn't completely encase a human like this armor fairy had.

Stolle gracefully bent her body this way and that.

"My mobility is so much better now!"

The cuirass was made of armor scales, so it wasn't restrictive like a rigid suit of armor.

"Lady Stolle, you should take a look at yourself in a mirror."

The maids brought in a full-length mirror and set it on the floor in front of Stolle.

"?!" Stolle froze in astonishment when she saw her helmet.

"I'll call Master Rodin and His Highness," one of the maids said, leaving the room just as Endelia returned with Mimachi.

Mimachi seemed…deflated, somehow, and quite gloomy. When she saw Stolle, she, too, was struck dumb.

"What do you think, Endelia? Isn't it exquisite?" Stolle asked.

"Who'd have guessed it was fairy armor?!"

"It's not only imbued with fairy blessings; there's more to it… It reminds me of the Realm Weaveguardian."

Who's that? I wondered. Did other fairy-birthing armors like this exist?

"It looks like House Menes's…" Endelia didn't finish, turning toward me, her eyes narrowed. "Lady Yui… Did you see it?"

I nodded, guessing that she meant the fairy.

Mimachi suddenly returned to her senses and pounced on Stolle.

"It's… It's just like in the legends of the Terra people! You're the Flower-Crowned Armor Maiden! Oh-ho-ho! So the stories were true!"

"What are you doing, Mimachi?! Hands off!"

"But where are your wings? In the legends, the Maiden can fly. I suppose that part was made-up…"

Well, she did have wings, but they were only visible to those with faysight. While Stolle might not be able to fly, if she ran really fast with those wings spread open, maybe she could glide?

Wait… This armor can float in the air!

Now that Stolle was wearing the armor properly, I could finally read the blessings woven into it.

The armor fairy was from a special tribe, but they also had elemental properties like regular fairies, and this one's seemed to be air and…heat? Once Stolle's affinity with the armor became sufficiently high, the fairy would not only be able to regulate temperature inside the armor but also conjure flame or icicle spears. It was like a set of magical armor straight out of a fantasy story.

Whoever had blesswoven this armor did an extraordinary job!

Much as it pained me to admit it, I knew I couldn't make anything like that. Not only because armorsmithing was beyond me, but even the level of craftsmanship that went into the blessed needlework exceeded my capabilities. It was quite an eye-opener—I'd thought I was good, but I had no inkling that it was possible to create fairies in this way.

I was almost certain now that people in this world had skill levels like in video games, and mine just wasn't high enough yet. That's why I could sense that I was missing something, even though I couldn't pinpoint what it was, exactly.

There was a knock at the door. I turned and saw Argit and Rodin enter the room again. They, too, gasped in admiration when they laid eyes on Stolle.

"Color me surprised. This is well beyond my expectations."

"If the legendary armor of House Menes really exists, perhaps its flame and ice javelins do, too?"

I suspected the javelins would materialize from the palm-length protrusions near the wrist joints on Stolle's gauntlets. Charged with magic, they would turn into full-length spears that detached from the armor. I wrote all this down on a piece of paper, which I then handed to Argit.

"What's this? Instructions for putting the armor on and…a note about its abilities?"

Argit went behind Stolle to look at her back. He gripped his forehead.

"Wings… The armor has fairy wings, like the Realm Weaveguardian."

"!! Your Highness, she has wings! Oooh!"

"M-Mimachi?! Y-you're scaring me!" Stolle cried. "That look in your eyes—it's unsettling, that pure, unadulterated adoration! What happened to your twisted, perverted side?!"

"Don't tell me off for admiring your armor! It's a masterpiece from Terra legends! If a blacksmith from my homeland saw you, they'd beg you to let them kiss your boots out of veneration! I'm not even joking!"

"So all Terra people are into bizarre kinks…?" Stolle whispered absentmindedly.

She was becoming quite prejudiced against the Terra people, basing her views entirely on Mimachi.

Hold on… I was under the impression that the Terra were something like hobbits, but maybe they were closer to dwarves? I'd love to meet a Terra craftsperson…provided they weren't really perverts, as Stolle feared.

"Stolle, read what Yui wrote here. Isn't it amazing?"

"Hmm? Oh, the armor can produce magical spears? It really is on par with the Realm Weaveguardian…?"

I noticed that Stolle was slowly beginning to lean to one side. It was all too much for her, and her mind was beginning to drift. Rodin caught her before she fell over.

"Stay focused, Stolle! You're on duty!"

"R-right!"

Stolle pulled herself together and stood up straight. She looked at the notes I wrote for her again. When she finished reading, she walked over to me, holding them close to her heart, and…she knelt on one knee in front of me.

"Lady Yui, I shall be forever grateful to you for revealing the secrets of my beloved armor. I swear to serve you loyally for as long as I live."

"Myah?!" I squeaked. Stolle's solemn oath made me feel the weight of responsibility as her mistress.

"Stolle, I think Lady Yui is feeling a little uneasy," Rodin said to her, and she raised her bowed head to look up at me. "Besides, haven't you already sworn to serve her?"

"Those two pledges differ in gravity! Lady Yui has proven that what we'd taken to be just a legend is in fact real, a real treasure passed down in my family. I'm no longer merely a knight hired to serve her, but her loyal protector!"

"Well, that's how you feel, but Lady Yui doesn't yet realize her position, and you're making her feel awkward. How about holding off on any grand declarations of allegiance until she's found her feet in her new role?" Mimachi suggested.

"But I—"

"Besides, once she marries His Highness, she'll be a member of the royal family, and you'll have to renew your vows anyway."

Stolle trembled slightly. And yet, despite the head-to-toe armor, I could tell from her eyes that she agreed with Mimachi.

But wait… Why was I being thanked so profusely? All I did was tell Stolle how to correctly wear the armor. It wasn't anything amazing. The people who made the armor—they were the geniuses, not me.

I wrote that on the notepaper and showed everyone around, but they only responded with patronizing smiles. I couldn't fathom why.

"With all that's been happening, I got held up here longer than I'd intended," said Argit. "I will have to see the head of House Menes on my

way back, as well as my son, and tell them about the Flower-Crowned Armor Maiden."

"Ah, indeed," Rodin replied, appearing distracted. "The head of House Menes—"

"I will caution him against coming to see Yui too soon, on account of her health. My son can meet her at the ball in three days. With Yui's talent, that should be enough time for her to make a dress."

"Yes, but what about court etiquette?"

"Her manners are impeccable. But dancing—that is probably out of the question. She's too frail to last even one song."

"This time, she will have to be excused from dancing."

"Nrrrh?"

A dress? Dancing at the royal court? I have to make a dress to wear at a ball?

"Lady Yui, will you be able to make a dress for yourself and a matching suit for His Highness for the ball? With blessings sewn in? You will have only three days," Rodin said, showing me three fingers for emphasis. "Make them as gorgeous as you possibly can," he added.

"Any...color...preference?" I asked, my voice still hoarse.

"You should avoid fresh green. That's His Highness's son's... The reigning king Amnart's color."

"Indeed," said Argit. "I prefer blue myself. To match the color of my magic, silver-blue."

Ah, so that's why he liked it. I sketched a few designs.

"Hmm. I like them. I will come for you in three days' time."

They took for granted that I'd be going to this ball... But, well, I was going to marry the former king, and I apparently possessed extraordinary skills, so I'd have to make my debut into high society sooner or later. It wouldn't be me whom Argit wanted to display, but my work—the blessed garments I was to make for the occasion.

I shuddered, thinking of how shameless my father was, calling himself an artisan while all he could produce were those pitiful rags. What he made and even his very existence itself were an affront to real seamstresses. I was outraged by how he disparaged needlework that did not transfer blessings onto garments, blind to how crude his clothes-making skills were. Someone needed to teach him a lesson.

Held by Stolle in her arms, I waved good-bye to Rodin and Argit, who were leaving for the capital. Once their horse-drawn carriage was out of sight, I wanted to get started with my work immediately, but I wasn't allowed. Maddeningly, I had to wait until the following day before working on my designs.

112

CHAPTER 6

Ball at the Royal Palace

The royal balls were different from the balls held by the nobility. The nobles' balls were banquets with a live orchestra and dancing, while the royal balls were quarterly events (held at the end of each season), which consisted of two parts: the Proclamations and the ball proper.

The Proclamations, which came before the ball, were where various important announcements were made: changes in nobles' or officials' rank; news about major accomplishments or cessation of prominent merchants' and artisans' businesses; marriages or deaths in the royal family.

Attendance at the ball in the royal gardens was optional, and socialites who hadn't been invited to the Proclamations could join as well to get the latest information and make connections. While there were always some artisans seeking patrons and merchants keen to find new business partners, it was largely a leisurely celebration for the aristocracy.

The Royal Palace grounds sprawled over an area comparable to a medium-sized village, and they comprised various offices and lodges of the top officials responsible for running the country, including Rodin's workplace and the workplace of his house staff. None of the buildings were more than three stories high, but they were quite expansive. Unlike in the neighboring countries, there was no sky-high palace.

Rodin entered the grounds through a different gate than usual, since this time he was not heading to work, but to the Proclamations.

"Rodin! Rodin!"

Recognizing the voice of a person he was hoping not to have to see that day, he heaved an annoyed sigh. Of course, since the event at the palace attracted a lot of nobles great and small, he knew that the other man might be there, too. At a glance, this man seemed like a pleasant, handsome fellow who could easily make young ladies swoon...but only to the ladies who didn't know him. The ones who did ignored him completely.

He and Rodin had been acquainted since their school years.

◆

The man was Nonnah of House Romiaccia, military consultants currently of the second rank, like Rodin. This musclebrain was a self-proclaimed best friend of Toluamia Mishutu, a first-rank noble and magic consultant.

Many children of nobles were sent to study at an academy from age twelve until sixteen, with the goal of making connections as much as acquiring education. That's where Rodin had become friends with Stolle Menes, Toluamia Mishutu, and the current king, Amnart. Nonnah Romiaccia had always been fifth-wheeling their friend group.

Rodin's rank at the time was quite low, but nobody tried to pick on him out of jealousy—his exceedingly good looks and impressive intelligence

helped him there. The one person who envied Rodin and held him in contempt was Nonnah.

Stolle was the only daughter of the head of the Menes family, who served as military advisers. Toluamia was a genius already nominated for the position of a magic consultant for the royal court. The serene and magnanimous yet also very smart Amnart was their junior, but he was already the king of the country.

In Nonnah's eyes, Rodin didn't fit in with that group. He was a far better match for them!

The five of them were often seen together, but they weren't a group of five friends. Nonnah wasn't as skilled in military arts as Stolle, and perhaps it was out of his sense of inferiority that he treated her with belligerence, mocking her armor and making sexist remarks.

Toluamia couldn't stand his guts and ignored him, but Nonnah was oblivious to his views about him and considered himself Toluamia's best friend.

Toluamia and Stolle tried their best to shield Amnart from Nonnah, who found it infuriating that the king favored Rodin over him.

Rodin was also often hanging out with his childhood friends Ulde and Skur, but they knew how to make themselves so inconspicuous with their first-class butler skills that most people didn't even register their presence.

◆

"Why, hello! How have you been?"

Nonnah came over with a lady in a stunning crimson dress holding his arm. He was grinning, so Rodin guessed he was going to tease him about something he'd discovered.

"I've been well, and I hope you have, too," Rodin replied politely, forcing himself to smile.

"I heard you've taken in the embarrassment of the Nuir family."

Caught off guard, Rodin frowned. Nonnah assumed he'd touched a nerve. He smiled wider. "You paid a pretty penny for her, isn't that so? Should've brought her here with you to show off your purchase."

"Of course he wouldn't bring her here. She's a servant now. Finally, a fitting position for her!" the woman at his arm chimed in, her voice coquettish. Rodin narrowed his eyes, trying to guess who she might be. She spoke as if she knew Yui.

"Excuse me, I don't think we've met before?"

"My name's Meilia Nuir. We don't look anything alike, of course, but I'm your servant girl's younger sister."

"Meilia…"

Nonnah spoke sharply, his smile vanishing. He wasn't liking the fact that his companion was making eyes at Rodin.

"Don't pout, Nonnah. You have to understand just how deeply grateful I am to Rodin for freeing us from the burden of looking after that good-for-nothing girl. And he even compensated us for her!"

"There seems to be a misunderstanding. I have paid a contract fee, which was to cover the expenses of the necessary arrangements. But I did not buy the girl."

Nonnah snorted.

"What expenses? You did them a favor by removing her from their household. They've been feeding her and putting a roof over her head all those years even though she can't blessweave."

Starving her rather than feeding her, Rodin thought, remembering how thin Yui was when he first saw her.

"I was very keen to have such a talented seamstress work for me."

"Talented? She can't blessweave."

At this point, Rodin was really struggling to keep a polite smile on his face. Nonnah didn't seem to know how infamous the Nuirs had become as of late. He'd always been deaf to the tone of those around him, and he tended to only pay attention to what interested him at the moment—which was usually digging up dirt on people. Rather than work on self-improvement, he preferred to find reasons to belittle others to make himself feel better. At his age, he was expected to become his father's aide, but he was still only a common knight.

Nonnah's father was a man deserving of respect. He would likely make his adoptive son, who was his current aide, the next head of the family.

The young man in question had a good character and was highly capable in his position. Since both he and Nonnah received the same upbringing, their father couldn't be to blame for how Nonnah had turned out. The Romiaccia family probably despaired over having such a wayward son.

Seeing as now he was associating himself with the Nuir family, he was a lost cause.

"Well, Mr. Nuir offered his other daughter to me, too, the one who could blessweave...but even the blessings couldn't compensate for her lack of skill with the needle."

At his tart remark, Meilia stopped looking at him dreamily, and instead, her face twisted in an ugly grimace.

"This... This is the height of rudeness! I've misjudged you, Mr. Calostira. You're an unrefined upstart, just like my father said! Nonnah, let's go. I've had enough of him!"

"R-right." Nonnah was a bit taken aback by her sudden flare of anger, but at the same time, seemed cheered up by her scorn for Rodin. They walked off.

Relieved to be freed of Nonnah earlier than expected, Rodin hurried his steps to the hall where the Proclamations were to take place.

The women Nonnah managed to persuade to accompany him on social occasions were never the type to be held in high esteem. Upsetting them was unlikely to lead to any repercussions. Rodin thought that offending Nonnah's girlfriends might be an efficient way to make the man leave him in peace.

••• CHAPTER 7 •••

Proclamations

I chose indigo as the base color for Argit's outfit. I embroidered it with silver thread and sewed on tiny but high-quality gemstone embellishments. The overall design was a cross between a tailcoat and a military uniform.

For myself, I made a simple dress in the same color. What was unique about it, though, was that it was minilength at the front but long and voluminous at the back. I would be wearing a lacy skirt underneath so that while my legs would be barely covered, they'd remain tantalizingly concealed.

I had to make my dress subtly sexy, lest people mistook me for a little girl due to my petite build and baby face. A deep décolletage was an option I didn't even consider, since my breasts were still rather small, so I made legs the focus. Yet, my legs were very thin, especially when seen from behind. I didn't have nice thighs to show off. *Voluptuous* wasn't an apt description of my body. That's why I wasn't showing much bare skin.

I did my best to make my outfit match Argit's, even though their designs were so different.

"Lady Yui, that's a marvelous dress!" Stolle exclaimed.

Her eyes had lit up the moment I started making it. She was into girly things like that, after all.

"Lady Stolle...would you let me...make you a...bridal gown?"

I wanted to do it someday, so I thought it'd be good to ask in advance.

"Oh, that's too kind an offer! Please don't waste your talent on me. I have my mother's dress, after all."

Pity. I was worried she might have an heirloom dress already, since it was customary to pass down bridal gowns in noble families. Stolle was so pretty, though, and she had a remarkably big bust, so I wanted to make her a dress that would be tailored to her...

"You sure you can fit in your mom's dress with those huge boobs of yours? Your mom wasn't a Menes, right?" Mimachi gestured in front of her chest to emphasize just how big Stolle's breasts were.

"Uh..."

Stolle pressed one hand to her chest piece, lost for words. Maybe it was her dream to wear her mother's dress for her wedding? Even though I couldn't see her face within her armor, her shock was palpable. I felt sad for her, but only for a moment, since this was my chance!

"I might—be able to...alter it...to fit you!"

"Oh?"

I would have to see it first to know for certain whether I could alter it, but I was quite confident given my current level of skill. But if it turned out that the dress wasn't suitable for alterations, I could make Stolle a brand-new one.

"Go marry someone, Stolle! Once it's just me and Lady Yui... Nya-ha-ha! We'll take baths together and sleep together! ♪"

"You think I could marry with a clear conscience, knowing you'd be left with Lady Yui without anyone to keep you in check?"

"Owww! Stolle, you're crushing my head! Your armor's powered up, remember? Ease up a little!"

With their banter in the background, I finished the outfits for the ball.

My dress had a motif based on the blue violet, a flower from this world. Between that and the makeup the maids brought me, I looked like an ephemeral being of an indecipherable age.

"You're as beautiful as a fairy, and I'm not trying to butter you up," Argit said when he came to take me to the ball. I was happy that I managed to impress him that much.

"Until...not so long ago...I was all skin and bones...dressed in rags." I spread my arms and spun around, making my dress flare out. "That's why...I don't think of myself...as pretty."

Oddly enough, although I hadn't grown accustomed to my new appearance, I could make clothes that suited it to perfection.

Argit, already changed into the outfit I had made for him, extended his arm toward me. I curtsied, as etiquette required, and let his big hand close over mine, small and fragile. We then got into a carriage. It was a few hours' journey to the capital.

We arrived a little while before the ball. Argit first took me to see the king. To my relief, Amnart wasn't wearing anything made by my father. Instead, he was dressed in clothes that had once belonged to one of his royal ancestors who was of a similar stature. The size was slightly off, but overall, the attire wasn't an eyesore like what Argit used to wear. On second thought, I shouldn't even compare anything to that slapdash patchwork of fabrics, which was a failure on so many levels, it didn't deserve to be considered clothing.

Unlike the slender Argit, Amnart was rather burly, but he made a warm impression. I'd say he reminded me of a lion—if lions were herbivores.

Three thrones had been set out in the room. The middle one was the most splendid. It was flanked by Amnart's throne and an empty one, reserved for the queen. The central throne was occupied by…a fairy the size of an adult human woman.

Their long hair was an obsidian black, with blue and red reflections, depending on the angle of light. Their eyes were green, but their color likewise seemed to grow darker or lighter depending on the angle. The fairy's white dress shimmered silver at times, only to appear golden the next moment, with the hem taking on a spring-leaf green. The dress was embellished with gemstones in the colors of ripe fruit. They wore accessories with flower motifs that might as well have been real fresh flowers—I couldn't tell.

"Oooh…"

I was staring at the fairy, spellbound. They smiled at me delicately. Joy and admiration made me feel warm inside, uplifted, as if I'd just seen the most beautiful rainbow.

My gaze then fell on the fairy's right hand…which was covered in terrible, putrid burns.

Poor thing! That looks so painful!

The sleeve of their dress didn't reach far enough to cover their sore hand, so I could see the full extent of the injury, down to the misshapen fingers. I remembered that fairies' wounds couldn't be healed in the same way as humans'.

I greeted King Amnart without taking my eyes off the fairy, then tugged at Argit's sleeve despite myself.

"Yui…," he said gently. He noticed what I was looking at.

"May I…make a glove…for the fairy?"

"If you can make one entirely out of strands of magic."

I spun my magic into a fine yarn, from which I made a lacy glove over

126

the fairy's injured hand, following one of the patterns I'd learned while I was confined to bed, recuperating.

"Oh!"

Everyone in the room who could see fairies gasped.

"Huh…," I muttered.

The tips of the glove got seared off. Was it because I didn't attach the glove to the fairy's clothing? Or was my skill level too low? Maybe the fairy had accepted the glove, but the burns flared up in reaction to it?

"Look! Her injury has healed ever so slightly!" Amnart exclaimed.

A young man—a magician, judging from his outfit—covered his quivering lips with his hand.

"We've tried to help her by offering her magic, but the curse would always prevail, repelling it," he said, his voice shaking as if he was about to cry.

"I knew if anyone could do it, it would be you, Yui," Argit told me, taking my hands into his and touching his forehead to them. His eyes were glistening with tears.

Those who did not have faysight looked around confused until someone whispered, "The Realm Weaveguardian…!" and then their expressions, too, changed to wonderment.

King Amnart agreed I should become the head of my family without the need to persuade him much. The position rightfully belonged to whoever was the most skilled at blessweaving. I also seemed to have scored points for being able to heal the Realm Weaveguardian—that, in fact, might have counted even more than my ability to perform blessweaving.

However, before my new status could be made official, I was to prove myself by winning a contest against my father. We all knew he wasn't the type to rescind his position without a fight.

"It is a great relief to see that there is an upstanding Nuir who can take the place as the head of the family," said Amnart. "I would have had no choice but to strip your family of their noble status in the near future, had things stayed the way they were."

I think that considering my home environment, I wouldn't have grown up to be "upstanding" as he said, had it not been for my memories from my past life. My younger sister had also been a perfectly nice person until she turned ten. She didn't like to study, but then again, many children don't.

This fairy, who was referred to as the Divine Fairy Cloth—or the Realm Weaveguardian—seemed to be of the same kind as the armor fairy I'd met before.

A large piece of tapestry covered the entire wall behind the thrones. That tapestry *was* the fairy.

I tried healing the fairy some more, hoping to gradually close her wounds, but when I reached out to her with my magic threads, the burn mark—the curse—used them to spread even further. I withdrew immediately, even before being instructed to stop.

"This is a living curse, you see," Amnart told me. "It's the manifestation of that woman's jealousy and obsession with my father."

Huh?

The fairy had been injured by Argit's jealous second wife.

"Does she...still have feelings...for you?" I asked Argit.

"Unfortunately. Our divorce was rather ugly."

"Normally, inflicting an injury upon the Realm Weaveguardian is punished with death," added Amnart. "The previous queen didn't cast a normal curse, though—she made a soul pact to harm the fairy. By killing her, we'd only risk the curse growing stronger."

*   *   *

Huh? Wait a minute…

Argit's ex-wife was madly jealous even of the fairies…and I'm now engaged to him.

Doesn't that mean…she'll want to curse me, too?

I shot Argit a fearful look. He must have guessed what I'd been thinking. It seemed that it hadn't occurred to him before that I'd be at risk, too. But, well, danger is a fact of life. Besides, his ex-wife had been exiled from the kingdom, so I was unlikely to ever meet her.

"I am so sorry… How unthinking I've been…"

He apologized to me, blood draining from his face.

I reflexively shook my head. Then I looked up into his eyes.

"Stolle and Mimachi will…protect me. I will…hone my ability…as a seamstress. I will be safe."

Over the past three days, I'd had many opportunities to witness Stolle's and Mimachi's battle abilities, and they were incredible indeed. Although, their reasons for fighting were…not worth mentioning.

Mimachi was an incredible and highly reliable maid when she was behaving…but the problem with her was that when she was unleashing her inner pervert, she was so crazy that this impression was what stuck in people's minds, overshadowing an appreciation of her abilities. I, though, completely trusted her to keep me safe. She might be a terrible pervert, but she was a royal maid all the same.

Stolle, my other guardian who kept Mimachi in check, was awe-inspiring all around.

"Thank you for allaying my fears, Yui," Argit said with a weary but kindly smile.

He was like a perfect loving dad character from the TV soaps I used to watch. Rodin sometimes made a similar expression, but he was more like a caring older-brother character given how young he was. I felt as if there was more depth in Argit's eyes when he looked at me, maybe because he actually was a father. In any case, his smile made me feel happy and protected.

While we were in our pleasant little bubble, the other people in the room seemed quite agitated. A few left in a hurry after Amnart told them something.

"First of all, we should see to it that Lady Yui becomes the official head of her family as soon as possible. The head of the family is granted several enhancements to their blessweaving as per the original contract with the spiders."

I opened my eyes wide at this revelation from Amnart.

"Enhancements? For the head of…family?" I asked.

Why had nobody told me about this before?

"Well, this is a matter for another time. Once new blessings are granted to you, I will ask you to have another attempt at healing the Realm Weaveguardian. For today, just enjoy the ball and the rest of the evening, Mother," Amnart said with an amicable laugh.

Once I married Argit, I would be Amnart's stepmom.

Argit had abdicated, so I wouldn't gain any governing power as his wife. Still, being his wife meant that the only person who would have authority over me would be Amnart. Even my own father would have no say over my life. Being called "Mother" by Amnart was reassuring—with him on my side, my safety was guaranteed.

Becoming the head of my family was such an alien idea to me, but Argit had set the gears in motion already so everything would be sorted out for

me. Personally, I was interested in the improvements to my blessweaving that came with this promotion more than any other consequences thereof. Maybe that was why Argit and Amnart were so keen on it, too—they were hoping that once I powered up, I would break the fairy's curse. That was my hope as well, and besides, I might finally unlock the abilities I sensed I was missing.

Amnart had actually chosen a lady to marry, and their engagement was going to be announced at that evening's Proclamations. That's why nobody put me forward as a candidate for his wife, although I could tell some people thought I'd be more suitable. Apparently, that would not be possible in any case, as the original pact with the spiders explicitly forbade the Nuirs from marrying the reigning king, although we were allowed to marry members of the royal family. It was a safety precaution, or so I was told.

Amnart's bride-to-be was to wear a blesswoven wedding dress. The pair had been waiting to announce their engagement so that they wouldn't be obliged to ask my father to make it. That's right—they asked me instead, and I gladly accepted!

Yay! I get to make a bridal gown! I'm going to give this my all!

I was so full of enthusiasm that I also offered to make an outfit for Amnart for the ball right then and there. The Royal Palace's seamstresses were flabbergasted the suggestion, but when they saw my finished work, they looked at me with reverence.

"It shouldn't be possible to sew an evening suit in under an hour! As far as we ordinary seamstresses are concerned, you're a goddess!"

"I knew how amazing Lady Yui was from the moment I saw Lady Stolle in her new armor! ★"

"You're as gifted as the legendary Founder, Yui!"

Amnart's companion fairy, who was a pretty spring-leaf green, helped me make his evening suit! And unlike most fairies, this one looked and acted like a full-grown woman!

After parting ways with Argit, whom I had been with since morning, I was to head to the party with Mimachi and Stolle, where we'd be joined by Rodin. We'd have dinner together, followed by the announcement of Amnart's engagement.

I'd been expecting to perhaps run into my father at the ball, but it was my sister I encountered first.

◆

"What's this supposed to be?"

We heard an agitated voice as we approached the entrance to the ball venue, which was something like a cross between an inner courtyard and a shrine I'd seen on TV in my past life. A row of pillars, decorated with colorful cloth wrapped around them, delineated the border of the semi-circular garden. There was only one wall, belonging to a different building, in front of which thrones had been placed. The king would presumably enter through the separate door next to the thrones. The open design of the space left nowhere for intruders to hide.

The woman whose shrill voice caught my attention was standing out of the way, not too far from the thrones but not too close to them, either. She was with a man, as well as another woman who caught my eye immediately— and wow, was this woman gorgeous! Her blond hair was wavily draped over her shoulders and back, made even more striking by the contrast with her crimson dress. No, I was doing her injustice by simply calling her hair blond—it was golden. Her features were so perfect that it was scary, her face

expressionless as she stared at the girl opposite her. She would probably look dazzling if she were smiling rather than glaring.

The girl the blond was mad at had red hair and rather thick, gaudy makeup. She was actually quite pretty, but her makeup was too caked-on to make that apparent, and the expression on her face was quite off-putting. And her dress…was the same color and in almost exactly the same design as the other lady's.

"Whatever do you mean?" she replied so nastily that I stopped in my tracks.

"Oh…"

I recognized that voice, ever so slightly jarring to my ears. And that hair color, too. The girl's features resembled my mother's… No, they were almost identical. Her tasteless makeup reminded me of my mother as well.

"Is something the matter, Lady Yui?" Stolle asked.

"Ah, I see. There's the other Nuir girl. You two look nothing alike," Mimachi said quietly.

"That's Lady Yui's sister?" Stolle looked from me to Meilia and back again.

"Lady Yui takes after the Founder, unlike this girl."

With all that makeup on, Meilia looked like a younger version of my mother.

We were standing on one of the paths in the garden, out in the open. Mimachi remarked that people could just get in from any side, really, but there was a designated entrance for the guests. The pillars, which looked like something taken out of an ancient shrine, cordoned off where the ball was taking place. They were draped in fabric.

Oh, this fabric is blesswoven, too.

Given the amount of skill involved, it must have been the work of a Nuir ancestor.

Ohhh, so the blessings provide a protective barrier. That's why there's a specified entrance.

The effect of the blessings seemed to be linked, but I could read what they did by looking at them from the outside.

"That beauty is none other than Hania from House Furke, the master dyers of noble rank!"

"Ah, yes! Those two both resemble the heir to House Furke!" Stolle replied cheerfully while grabbing Mimachi's head to stop the almost drooling pervy maid from doing anything silly.

I gathered that this Hania and her brother (?) were a big deal.

"Do you have no pride as an artisan?"

"Ooh, are you trying to intimidate me? What are you blathering on about? I'm not some artisan; I'm a noblewoman!" my sister replied, sidling closer to the knight (?) who was with them, a glass with some beverage in her hand.

What she had said riled me. We Nuirs were artisan nobles, and being a master-class artisan was even more of a reason to feel proud than being of aristocratic descent. Yet my sister looked down on artisans!

"Hey, miss, stop picking on my friend, will you?"

The knight accompanying my sister butted in on the conversation, trying to act like he was above all this even though he'd been captivated by Hania earlier.

He was good-looking but didn't seem very likable. Hania completely ignored him, which ticked him off. I recognized the mannerisms of someone who assumed everyone owed them the utmost respect. Arrogance was painted on his face. Perhaps that's why, to me, his good looks seemed somewhat pitiful, wasted.

He made a good match for my sister.

*　　*　　*

Had enough of Rodin, Meilia? This man is a pretty poor substitute, though.

At least Stolle is here. She'll be enough of a deterrent to keep Meilia from trying to start anything with me.

"I'm fairly confident that's the dress we sent to your family for the blessings," Hania said to Meilia.

...

......

....

...Theft? Seriously, Meilia?

My head spun; I was so angry, embarrassed, and disgusted with my sister. Over the past five years, she'd become so much like my parents. Any remnants of sisterly affection toward her vanished as if with a snap of fingers.

Hania was absolutely correct, and nothing Meilia could say in her defense would have convinced me otherwise. The size of the dress was exactly right for her. Slight alterations had been made to make it fit my sister, but it was too tight at the waist. Meilia was wearing her corset unnaturally tight. Her bust was sticking out in an odd shape. I guessed she had padded it.

"My family chose that dress color especially for this day," said Hania. "You go and change into something else."

"Who do you think you're talking to? I'm the heir to House Nuir. Don't you even try to send us more dresses for blessings—I won't accept them! *You're* the one who should change into something else!" Meilia shouted before emptying the contents of her glass onto Hania's dress.

"How dare you!"

"Hmph! That dress was too good for you anyway, you low-ranking wench!"

I saw red.

"Let's…go inside," I urged.

"Lady Yui, you weren't thinking about sewing blessings into that lady's dress, were you?" Stolle asked me sternly.

I cocked my head. "May I—not…?"

The hem of Hania's dress had gotten splashed. I thought I could ask the fairies to help me dry the stain, and if any discoloration was left, I would embroider over it.

Hania's dress seemed to have been made in a hurry, while the one my sister was wearing looked more sophisticated. My family were horrible people, but even I wouldn't have guessed they'd go as far as to steal a dress they'd been commissioned to blessweave, replacing it with an inferior product.

I felt so sorry for Hania, who'd been wearing a poor copy of her original dress, which had now been dirtied by the shameless thief. Something had to be done about this!

"I want to…embroider the dress…complementing…that color."

"But the plan was to wait on revealing your abilities until His Highness and His Majesty made their appearance, wearing the clothes you made for them."

I hadn't forgotten about that, of course…

"But…I can't ignore…what she did…"

Tears streamed down my cheeks.

"Let her do it, Stolle. It's totally justified in this case."

"But, Mimachi—"

"Hania's the queen-to-be," Mimachi whispered.

*   *   *

Stolle picked me up in her arms.

How did Mimachi find out that info? I wondered.

"Mimachi, it's on you to report this."

"Sure."

With that, my gallant knight in her dazzling armor carried me into the garden where the ball was to take place. I stuck out like a sore thumb.

◆

By the time we made our way inside, my sister and her companion had already walked off elsewhere. Hania stood there alone, holding up the edge of her dress to conceal the wet part of the hem. It was as if there was an invisible wall around her. Even the men didn't try talking to her about the mean Nuir girl.

"Why is...everybody...shunning her?"

"It's because of Nonnah. That repulsive reject is the eldest son of the head of the Romiaccia family, and he's very persistent about trying to get back at people he thinks insulted him in some way," Stolle said with more venom in her quiet voice than Mimachi could muster when she was spouting invectives.

I hadn't heard of the Romiaccias before, but I guessed they were high-standing nobles. Nonnah was on track to being disowned, according to Stolle. What a fine partner for my sister.

"You...know him?" I asked.

"..."

Stolle was silent for a while. Apparently, she hated his guts so much that she didn't even want to admit to knowing him.

"I've known him for some time, as a rotten person making the air stink wherever he goes."

Sheesh, Stolle can be so scary!

Her tone was lighthearted and sweet, yet as menacing as if she were chanting a curse. She was basically saying this guy should drop dead!

Stolle kept walking with me on her shoulder while we were talking, with people turning to look at us as we passed by, until we arrived in front of Hania.

"Greetings, Lady Hania of House Furke." Stolle knelt, setting me down beside her.

A flame fairy who had been protectively cuddling Hania looked at us, and their eyes lit up.

That's a powerful guardian fairy!

It seemed that one of the effects of the magical barrier around the garden was to make fairies invisible to those outside. That's why I hadn't noticed any before!

This fairy specialized in fire, and they were unusually big, like Amnart's. Now I understood that Hania's dress had been designed to match her fairy!

Suddenly, Amnart's fairy appeared beside us with a flutter, carrying a bundle of Amnart's magic. Several men turned to look at us in surprise; they must have possessed faysight.

"Oh? What's Am's guardian fairy doing here...?" Hania said quietly to herself. I guessed Am was her pet name for Amnart.

His fairy smiled, crinkling their eyes. They then absorbed the bundle of magic, which they spun into thread and offered to me. Mimachi must have been very quick with letting the royals know what was going on here.

"You can also see fairies?" Hania asked me.

"Yes. I will...mend your dress. It seems—the fairy...wants me to use... the king's magic for it."

One end of the fairy's thread stretched toward my spider's belly, while the other went to the flame fairy. They peered into the flame fairy's face questioningly, who in turn nodded resolutely to show their permission.

"I'm...Yui. The Maiden of the Needle."

I took a needle out of a case Stolle had been carrying for me, and I threaded it with a spring-green thread from my spider. Next, I conjured another "hand" out of my magic and made for it a magical needle to hold, threading it with Amnart's silky magic, imbued with the power of the flame fairy. I had a hunch that I would have to work both threads simultaneously.

Fire does not merely burn.

Fire also gives us light. The sun is a ball of fire, and its sunshine nourishes plants.
Absorbing the green magic, the flame fairy grew stronger.

Green vines crept up the crimson dress, unfurling dozens of leaves. Twisting around Hania. Protectively, lovingly.
Hee-hee—this thread contains magic from Amnart, who's crazy about her!
The embroidered greenery sucked up the moisture from the part of the dress that had been splashed with the drink, covering the hem.
"Incredible...," said Hania. "You sewed with two needles at once..."
It was the first time I'd tried it. The pattern I was embroidering was symmetrical, so it wasn't that hard for me to sew in parallel.
The bottom part of the dress was the one that had an unfinished look to it before, so I took care of that as well.
"Whew... All done," I said.

"It's as if you were the reincarnation of the first Nuir! Your blessweaving is marvelous! You did it so quickly, as if by magic!"

Well, as far as I know, I'm just the reincarnation of an ordinary girl from Japan.

Hania's fairy hugged her happily, smiling at her broadly. Hania returned the smile.

Wow! With that smile, she was even cuter and more beautiful than I'd imagined! Her smile dazzled everyone, me included. In fact, I was even more dazzled, since I could see her fairy as well.

Hania then smiled at me. "Thank you! Might I trouble you with a request? I'd like to do something for them in return for their help."

She produced a cluster of magic so big that she had to hold it in both arms. She handed it to the fairies, and they absorbed it and spun threads for me.

"With this much...I could make...a flower for the king—and one for his fairy."

"That would be lovely!"

I made two crimson flowers in lace. One bloomed on the chest of the green fairy, and the other in Hania's hand.

"They're beautiful."

"Lady Yui, I've brought you a drink."

Mimachi had appeared out of nowhere to offer me a cup of a warm drink in the manner of a top maid. It tasted like the honey-and-yuzu citrus drink I remembered from my past life. It soothed my throat.

At this rate, I was going to become a connoisseur of all the foods and drinks in the kingdom that were good for sore throats.

"His Majesty and His Highness will be here soon. Lady Hania, Lady Yui, please come with me."

Mimachi gestured toward the thrones, and the crowd parted for us.

It was like magic. Some people took interest and tried to approach us, but Mimachi indicated to them that we had some connection to the king, and they left us alone as we made our way to the thrones.

By then, we were the focus of attention. I overheard people whispering about "the Founder," about rebirth. Nobody seemed to recognize me as the discarded oldest daughter of the Nuir family, even though it should have been obvious who I was, since only the Nuirs could blessweave. Mimachi noticed my confused expression.

"Your talent and beauty are so far removed from the current generation of Nuirs that it seems impossible for you to be one of them."

"Indeed," Stolle agreed.

"?" Hania cocked her head. "I'd believe it if you told me she was the Founder reborn."

"She's currently under the guardianship of Rodin Calostira. His Highness Argit bestowed upon her the title of Maiden of the Needle. Ah, I should introduce myself, too, I suppose. I am Stolle Menes, Lady Yui's knight."

"But then what is Lady Yui's current family status?"

"A former Nuir? Hmm, it makes more sense to present her as a reincarnation of the Founder! ☆"

But I'm just the reincarnation of a normal Japanese girl!

There is no shortage of legends about fairies acquiring a human form and secretly living among humans thereafter. Many of the attendees at the royal ball that day thought that they witnessed such a being.

Members of chivalrous orders and people of Terra descent immediately

identified Stolle in her stunning armor as the Flower-Crowned Armor Maiden from the legends of House Menes. To them, the girl carried by the Armor Maiden could be none other than a fairy in human form.

Silver hair, golden eyes...

The girl had a childlike beauty, but her manner was that of an adult, world-wise woman. Her age was impossible to guess, which contributed to the impression that she was really a fairy rather than an ordinary human.

A knight was carrying her on her shoulder—and such a thing at the royal ball required explicit permission from the king. Who could it be, carried by a knight in her full armor? Many of the assembled were convinced it had to be the king's bride-to-be.

The girl and her knight first approached Hania Furke, who'd just had an altercation with another lady and her companion. Those who had been concerned for Hania but too intimidated by her extraordinary beauty to talk to her were relieved that the fay girl seemed to be sympathetic toward Hania. Having the girl show Hania her favor would make her feel better, they thought. But the girl did far more than just offer a kind word.

Even among the king's closest associates, not many possessed faysight, so only a handful of people were able to witness what exactly the girl did for Hania. Those of them who knew a thing or two about magic were shocked by what they saw.

The ability to manipulate magic was what made one a magician, although all they needed for their craft to work was to wield magic like a pencil to draw magic circles with. Even the most outstanding magicians could only use chunks of magic as thick as an adult man's arm, and consequently, magic circles, which were essential to conveying the magician's requests to fairies, had to be drawn very big. Meanwhile, this girl was freely manipulating thread-thin strands of magic.

Both the faysighted and those who were sensitive to magic gasped.

"She has the power of the Founder..."

"Is she her, reborn...?"

People were speaking their thoughts out loud without realizing, mesmerized by the scene straight out of a fairy tale. She had to be either the Founder, or a fairy in human form.

When a smile returned to Hania's face, people wondered if she, too, was a fairy incarnate. Her beauty shone spectacularly once she finally showed emotion.

Many men were absolutely smitten with the two women at that moment, but they could tell that these ladies were not meant for them. When the Flower-Crowned Armor Maiden and the Terra maid indicated for the crowd to make way, they stood aside, knowing that was the most they could do for them.

◆

In this kingdom, women with faysight became candidates for royal spouses.

The sixteen-year-old Hania had kept her ability to see magic and fairies secret until the day of that royal ball.

Hania's family were nobility, but her father was an artisan to the core, completely devoted to his work. He left the matters of the household entirely to his wife.

Hania could vaguely remember her mother, who of course had noticed early on that her daughter had faysight, instructing her at age three not to tell anyone about her ability until she was grown-up. Her mother wanted to protect her from high-ranking nobles vying to snatch her or embroil her in

their own political ploys. She was planning to give Hania the education she would need later in life, when the public would have learned of her power. Alas, she succumbed to illness and died while Hania was still little.

Her bereaved father was at a complete loss without his wife. All he knew was his craft, at which he excelled, but he couldn't run a household. It fell to Hania's older brother to manage the land the family owned while the servants looked after her. It worked for a while…until their relatives sent their own servants to "help out" and Hania acquired a new mother.

Hania's distraught father remarried out of desperation and delegated the supervision of their land to the servants provided by his relatives.

He didn't know that his still-underage son was extraordinarily talented. He didn't know that his old servants had been raising Hania with genuine love and care.

And so their estate was nearly eviscerated by the selfish, luxury-demanding woman who became his second wife; the greedy relatives seeking to get as much as they could for themselves; and the new unscrupulous servants who were carrying out their orders.

Had Hania's brother not received help from his friends and their guardians, Hania, whose days had been filled with growing resentment for her shameless, manipulative stepmother, would have probably grown up unable to experience love.

Both Hania and her brother inherited their mother's looks, but Hania was much more like their father in personality.

A year after their father's remarriage, their rank fell by one grade, but then Hania's father made a comeback as an artisan, while her brother effectively took over as the head of the family and, helped by his more experienced friends, got their estate back in order.

Then one day, a boy came to stay at their house for some time. He'd play with Hania or share his knowledge with her. His mother wasn't good to him, either, so he could understand what Hania had been going through with her stepmother. Even though he was older than her, he treated her as his peer, and the two of them got along.

The Furkes' house was one of his temporary homes where his father sent him to keep him safe from his second wife, a princess from another country, rendered insane by jealousy. The boy's name was Amnart, and he was the crown prince.

◆

Hania smiled, holding the lacy rose imbued with fire magic. She gave it to King Amnart, who planted a kiss on it.

He then placed it on his chest, matching his fairy... Well, not quite. He stuck it under the clasp of his cloak, so it was more or less at the same position.

◆

When Amnart first met Hania, she had seemed dead inside. He actually felt repulsed by her, since she reminded him of his biological mother, the one who had depended on her elderly nurse for everything.

An elderly woman with a sinister fire in her eyes grabbed little Amnart by his arm and yanked him toward his expressionless mother. Amnart's royal guard quickly pushed her away.

"How dare you touch His Highness!"

It was shocking that the woman would do that. Only Amnart's father,

the king, was allowed to touch the boy without asking for permission. Amnart was the crown prince, after all.

Although at that point, he was only a little boy, and everybody thought his chances to succeed the throne were slim, on account of his father being so young and in robust health. Everyone—Amnart included—assumed that by the time Argit decided to step down, the crown would be passed on to Amnart's son, should he have any.

But even if he didn't become king himself, the boy had to be protected, so that one day he could become the father of the next ruler. It was very clear by then that Argit wasn't going to have more children with his then-wife.

Amnart's mother should have done something to stop the old woman from approaching the boy, or she should have rebuked her for what she'd done. But she did nothing, staring at her nails as if unaware of what was going on around her.

That sight left a deep impression on Amnart. He became disillusioned about his mother and ended his very brief period of that optimistic childhood naïveté. In a sense, his mother was a good example—an example of the sort of people to avoid at all costs. He acquired a disgust for people who had no will of their own, doing what others told them like mindless puppets. That's not to say he didn't also feel pity for them.

When he first saw Hania, she appeared to be just like his mother, so he initially felt a strong dislike toward her.

"Can I help you?"
"We're friends of Ian Furke. We've come to see him."

Upon hearing that, Hania livened up, and she no longer looked like Amnart's mother. Her pale cheeks took on color, and her eyes sparkled with hope. It was like watching a tightly closed bud unfurl into a blossom. The transformation completely changed Amnart's impression of her, and it also taught him that beauty was not defined so much by the features one was born with but by the expression on their face.

"You know my brother?"

"Indeed, we do. My name is Rodin Calostira."

"And I'm Am Lomelo."

The young prince had to keep his true identity secret.

The little Hania, dressed in ill-fitting servant's clothes, curtsied and replied politely:

"Welcome to our residence. My name is Hania Furke. I'm afraid my brother is…" She looked up at the attic. Ian was being kept under lock and key there in an attempt to break his spirit and have the handsome boy serve the interests of the calculating relatives of the family.

"Yes, we know. We're here to help him, actually."

Amnart couldn't bear to see Hania's face cloud over with worry again, the light disappear from her eyes. Perhaps that was when he first sensed the possibility that one day he might fall in love with her.

No sooner had Ian been set free than he went to see his father, whom he found to have given in, letting the relatives and his wife dictate what he should do, without the courage to resist. What Ian did was beat sense into him, literally.

While Ian was well-disposed and shy, his martial-arts abilities were on par with masters in the field. Had his sister not been held hostage, he'd have single-handedly driven out the evil servants and his stepmother from their estate.

When Hania saw her delicate-looking brother knock out even a burly Terra with one blow, she decided to study martial arts herself, not willing to

be a defenseless damsel having to rely on others. As a result, she gained both confidence and some muscle, which Amnart found quite appealing.

And so Amnart and Hania became friends.

His first impression of her was unfavorable, but she later became his first friend who was younger than him. He treated her with fondness, as if she were his little sister.

Amnart witnessed his stepmother losing her mind from jealousy. Thinking that one day he would have to marry a faysighted woman to sire the next royal generation filled him with apprehension and despair.

Children who can see fairies generally have a natural propensity to grow up to be kind and righteous. Through contact with fairies, they learn how to be caring toward those who are smaller and weaker.

Amnart's biological mother and stepmother both were exceptions in that matter. Argit didn't have much of a choice regarding who to marry, since there were few faysighted women at the time.

But then…Amnart discovered one at a residence where he'd been staying undercover. It was Hania Furke.

When he noticed her ability, he felt a mixture of hope and terror. Had her talents become known, she'd be at risk from the madly jealous queen. Or his father, who was still a young man, might choose to remarry, taking her as his wife. Amnart realized that he wanted to protect her from both scenarios.

And that was because he'd fallen in love with her. She, too, didn't see him as another brother figure in her life but loved him as a man.

◆

"I, Amnart Lomestometlo, hereby ask you—Hania Furke, Maiden of the Flame—for your hand in marriage!"

At his proclamation, the lacy rose quivered like flames, the vines embroidered on the hem of his cloak bursting into flowers and buds. A blessed garment gaining new blessings—a miracle.

Amnart smiled with one half of his mouth. There was no longer any need to hold a contest between Yui and her father after those gathered at the ball witnessed her blessweave Hania's dress and the incredible transformation of the rose.

"This young seamstress has proven beyond doubt that the title of the head of House Nuir rightfully belongs to her. I hereby proclaim her the head of House Nuir, and I grant permission for her marriage to my father, Argit Lomestometlo!"

◆

That caused quite a stir.

For one, I was appointed the head of the Nuirs without having to best my father in a contest.

I was actually thrown by Amnart's unexpected announcement.

"You've already shown them that you're the best! ★" Mimachi whispered to me with a wink.

"Only a fool would lodge a complaint with the king after your display

of skill," Stolle said coldly, her gaze fixed on a fat man who was making his way toward the platform with the thrones.

"Your Majesty! I would advise you against making such hasty decisions!" the man shouted as the royal guards stopped him from getting too close to the king.

In the few months—or had it been half a year already? In any case, he'd put on a *lot* of weight since I'd last seen him. His face was reddened from anger, and the boils on his face looked ready to burst. Gross.

"*I* am the head of House Nuir!" he shouted. "This girl doesn't deserve the title!"

A faint shadow of irritation colored Amnart's placid countenance.

"As the former head of House Nuir, you should know very well that this title belongs by right to whoever is the most accomplished at blessweaving."

"But, Your Majesty! The title can only be granted to a member of the Nuir family! Not some girl of unknown pedigree!" His voice broke into an ear-piercing falsetto.

Wait… Does he not recognize his own daughter?

I stared at him in disbelief. Argit wrapped his arm around me and picked me up.

"Do you consider my Maiden of the Needle unsuitable?" Argit asked, holding me securely.

My father was so agitated, he gasped for air, his face turning purple. He couldn't just openly insult the former king's fiancée.

"Can you not tell from her features that she comes from a bloodline related to the royal family?" Argit continued.

Huh? Is he not going to tell my father that it's me, Yui? Perhaps he wants to avoid that in case my father tries to lay some claims to me, despite having disowned me in all but name.

"Or are you prepared to prove to us that your ability is superior to hers?

As it happens, it would appear that your younger daughter is wearing a dress with an uncanny resemblance to Lady Hania's. Why don't you sew blessings into it, so that we may compare the outcome?"

Oof—the biting irony in his voice!

"I…I don't have my spider with me tonight," my father, whose name I realized I didn't know, replied shakily. He began to sweat profusely, and his eyes darted this way and that wildly.

If Argit was an agility-type character, Amnart was a power-type. Amnart was normally calm and self-assured, but when angered, he could be very intimidating…as he was now, addressing my father coldly.

"You will return the dress your younger daughter is wearing to the Furke family at once. If you still wish to dispute the transfer of the title of head of House Nuir, you have until the end of tomorrow to present a blessed dress of your own making that would surpass the one my fiancée is wearing at the moment."

The king would not give any more time to my father, so he waved him away. Royal guards immediately surrounded my father, and when he loudly resisted, they knocked him unconscious and carried him away.

The guards led my sister away, too. A knight who appeared to be their captain appeared beside the man who'd been accompanying Meilia and took him away as well.

The artisan nobles are respected only as long as their skills meet the expected standards. Should they fail to deliver, they lose their special privileges, as this event clearly illustrated.

And that caused yet another stir—the blessweaving, that is.

While most of the people in the room had no way of knowing this, I had made the outfit the king was wearing on that occasion. Once I finished sewing,

fastening off the thread and cutting it, the effect of the blessing granted the wearer invulnerability to attacks. The cloak likewise became indestructible. That's why I didn't think it possible for the blessing within it to merge with another, but that's what happened when the two high-level fairies joined forces.

By fusing their powers, the fairies triggered an extremely rare phenomenon—the birth of a fairy, not in the way it naturally happened, but through their volition. Would the newly created fairy turn the cloak into fairy armor once they awakened? It seemed as if it would take some time for this to occur, on account of my thread being too low-level.

It dawned on me then what it was that I felt I'd been missing. I wasn't the only one still lacking in skill—my spider's thread was low-level, too!

Come to think of it, I only began using my spider's thread for the blessweaving after moving in with Rodin.

If I was to cure the Realm Weaveguardian, I needed to raise my spider's level and get the fairies who created her to come help by contributing a little of their power. Perhaps the tapestry itself had to be mended at the same time.

My spider would need to become as powerful as the first spider of the Nuirs, which had turned from a monster into a divine beast... And how many high-level fairies had lent their power to make the tapestry that protected the entire kingdom with a magical barrier? Five, eight? This would be a tall order, one verging on the impossible...

Amnart and Hania danced to one song before bidding everyone a good evening and leaving the garden. My companions and I were then led to the same audience hall where we'd spoken with the king earlier.

The same people as before were there again. I shared my thoughts with them. The news that the king's cloak may turn into fairy armor was greeted with excitement...while my theory as to what was needed for the Realm Weaveguardian's recovery didn't inspire as much optimism.

"We must not delay Yui's advancement to the head of House Nuir," Amnart said with renewed resolve.

Nobody present voiced an objection, even though right up to the ball, the plan was for the king to confiscate the Nuirs' land and transfer its ownership to House Menes.

I noticed a few people frowned, but even they remained silent. They could be divided into three categories.

The first group was keen on reducing the power and influence of the royals over the nobles.

The second group comprised rivals of House Menes.

The third group had been receiving bribes from House Nuir.

Mimachi whispered into my ear that we needed to be careful, because despite not challenging the king openly, there were quite a few powerful people here who disagreed with his decision.

"I don't think anyone sane would try to side with that despicable man at this point," said Stolle.

"It riles some pathetic people that Lady Yui is so young but already so amazing," added Mimachi.

"I would expect supporters of Yui's father to also be appreciative of the garments he makes. Perhaps we should make it a condition that if they were to cast their votes for him, they would be obligated to wear only clothes made by him for the rest of their days."

Argit's suggestion was so cruel! But he'd been wearing those grotesque outfits for most of his life… Thinking about it brought tears to my eyes.

I noticed that some of the people who were close enough to overhear our conversation had gone pale.

"From…now on—I will make…any garment you require, Your Highness," I said to Argit, shyly tugging at his sleeve.

As he turned toward me, his gaze softened once more. He put his large hand on my head and stroked my hair.

"I will greatly appreciate that, my Maiden of the Needle."

◆

An ornate chest was brought into the room. Inside was a large piece of fabric.

"This is the original pact between the first spider and the founder of the Nuir family."

I recognized that this fabric, with a magic circle drawn in the middle, was an enchanted tool for those who could perform blessweaving.

"Place your spider at the center."

I did as Amnart said. Slowly, my spider began to glow silver.

"It's the color of Yui's magic," Argit noted, and a murmur went through the small crowd gathered around us.

"So beautiful," came whispers from all around. The light must have been visible to everyone, not only to those with faysight.

"Oh…"

Letters started appearing in the air, spiraling outward from the magic circle. I followed them with my eyes.

"I, King Amnart of House Lomestometlo, proclaim that the ancient pact has been renewed!"

The letters began turning pale pink in counterclockwise. It was a very old text, and some of the archaic spellings eluded me.

"The pink letters are in the color of the Founder's magic," Argit explained. "The text reads, 'I, the Black-Haired Maiden Sakura, and the Spider Maiden hereby pledge to be bound by ties of friendship forever after.' The golden letters after 'Spider Maiden' are the name of the original spider. Nobody can read it."

My eyes were glued to the golden katakana characters. The Founder's name was Sakura, even though there were no cherry blossom trees in this world. There was only a climbing plant named blossom, with flowers that looked exactly like cherry blossoms.

Some of the animals and plants in this world resembled ones I knew from my past life, and their names likewise were similar if not the same...

There was no reason to think that I was the only person reincarnated from a different world. The Founder had written the spider's name in katakana! She had to be from the same world as me!

"When monsters reproduce, their offspring are all clones of the parent. Only in exceptional circumstances may they become new beings. Nuirs' spiders are not given names because they all already have a name."

So that's why!

In the Nuir household, my only friends were the fairies and my spider, so of course I wanted to give it a name. But no matter how many times I tried, I couldn't. Whenever I came up with a name for it, I'd soon realize I'd forgotten what it was. After many tries, I finally gave up. Now I finally knew why no name actually stuck!

Ever since the original spider evolved from monster to divine beast, her consciousness continued to live on, passed down from parent spider to offspring. Did my spider still retain all those memories? Did this kind of existence cause it suffering?

*   *   *

"Yui Nuir, Maiden of the Needle—raise your hand."

I raised my hand and held it over my spider as I was told.

"Repeat after me: 'I pledge my everlasting friendship to you and fairy-kind, O Spider Maiden.'"

"I pledge my…everlasting friendship…to you and fairy-kind…O Spider Maiden…"

Would the Spider Maiden react if I called her by her name? I was burning with curiosity. The Founder was the only other Japanese person I knew of in this world, and she was my ancestor! How I wished I could meet her!

"O Spider Maiden…Ariadne!"

I sensed that everyone in the room had looked at me in astonishment, but I wouldn't take my eyes off the magic circle, which began transforming.

My silver magic changed consistency, becoming like cotton candy. And then it began to turn golden. My spider folded up its legs, making itself look small. The light of my magic enveloped it. I quickly withdrew my hand.

"Wh-what's happening?"

"The golden magic belongs to the divine beast…"

"Did she…? Did she manage to read the divine beast's name…?"

Argit and Amnart stepped away from the pact while the crowd whispered in alarm. A young magician scraped the floor by the table with his magic staff, drawing a circle around us.

"Your Majesty! Your Highness! Lady Yui! Step out of the magic circle!"

Argit tried to pick me up to carry me there, but…

"Oh…"

…I began floating.

"The pact!"

"Close the magic circle, Toluamia! We'll be fine!" Amnart shouted.

"Ngh…"

The magician Toluamia closed the circle with effort. As soon as he did so, a mass of golden filaments of magic spread out from the pact, and I, Amnart, and Argit were lifted into the air. The magic circle filled with golden threads. Besides me and the two kings, Stolle and Mimachi were also inside the circle, and Hania slipped in quickly while there was an opening. Our fairy familiars were with us, too, of course. I noticed that Amnart's royal guard and an elderly butler also ended up inside.

"To think so much condensed magic had been lying dormant inside the pact…"

"Toluamia was right to enclose the pact within a magic circle. Exposure to such power might hurt those unaccustomed to magic."

"Am!" Hania called out to the king, brushing magic threads aside as she found her way toward him.

"Hania? Did you sneak inside?"

"I had to. I'm your fiancée, and the more people you have to guard you, the better, isn't it?"

The look in Hania's eyes left no room for discussion. Amnart swallowed words of rebuke, sighing.

"You shall have to assign a royal guard to our queen as soon as possible," Argit said to him. Amnart smiled wryly and nodded.

I heard later that being the one who was protected by others rather than the other way around was essential to the king's role. That's why, even

though Amnart would have preferred to be the one to keep his beloved safe, he couldn't deny her decision to be his protector—much to his frustration.

Meanwhile, a cocoon so large that a person could fit within appeared on the table. It began to make crinkling noises as it slowly split open.

I saw an alabaster-skinned back. Next, long, golden hair. If the being that was emerging from the cocoon had wings, I'd have thought she was a fairy. She did not have wings, though she did have eight spider legs. She had white fur on her lower body (although it was a spider body, it was densely covered in soft hair, which looked just like fur), with golden lines and patches making a mysterious pattern.

"Aaah! That was a long nap."

The Spider Maiden stretched with a yawn. Her upper body was so beautiful, she could be a goddess of light.

She smiled. *"Hi there! You called me by my name, so you must be an otherworlder, too, huh?"*

She spoke to me in Japanese, which I hadn't heard since my rebirth.

Suddenly, golden threads shot out toward me and snatched me from Argit's side.

"Yui!"

He tried to reach for me, but the golden threads formed a wall, separating me from the rest of the group.

It was like a cocoon, with me and Ariadne inside. It was quiet there, all external sounds blocked.

"Now, tell me your name."

Her eyes were a uniform pale pink like two rose-quartz gemstones, without whites or darker pupils. When they met mine, I felt pins and needles in my body, but it wasn't an unpleasant sensation. It was quite relaxing, like having a massage.

*   *   *

"My name is Yui. In my past life...I was called Tsumugi."

I was surprised at how easily Japanese came back to me.

"Nice to meet you, even though our acquaintance will be very brief. My name's Ariadne. In my past life, I was called Aria."

"Wait—why are you saying...our acquaintance will be...brief?"

"Perhaps you know this about monsters already, but our consciousness is transferred to our offspring. Although, most monsters don't really possess a consciousness, acting purely on instinct." She thought for a while and shook her head. *"In a way, monsters are a by-product of consciousness."*

Ariadne twirled her fingers in the air and conjured an image—it was human-shaped, almost like a gingerbread cookie, and it emanated dark miasma. The miasma thickened, forming eggs...out of which spiders hatched.

"That's how the system works in this world. Humans' negative emotions give birth to monsters."

"When you call it a system, it sounds...as if someone...designed it that way...," I remarked, and Ariadne clapped her hands.

"That's exactly what happened. This world is designed by humans. Humans are gods here. But when human psyches break, so does this world, and that happened many times over... All those negative emotions turned into monsters."

"What? Humans...are gods?" I asked incredulously.

I'd never actually thought that this world might have any gods. There were fairies and apparently levels for abilities like sewing, but...people being gods?

"The world has become so unstable that it stopped choosing native humans with divine powers. Instead, it brings over people from another world...the one where we used to live. That's why we were transmigrated here. This extraordinary

phenomenon occurred multiple times because a passage has opened between the two worlds." Ariadne narrowed her eyes. *"It seems magic has fallen into a decline while I was sleeping."*

"Magic?"

"Like I said, this world is shaped by the will of humans. The will of many humans becomes crystallized as magic."

"Their will...becomes magic..."

"The person from Earth who created the current version of this world based it on video games, hoping to stop the vicious circle of humans creating worlds that only led to the humans' destruction. This person's system turns negative emotions into monsters, which can then be slain to restore balance." Ariadne giggled. *"But that's no use. The fairies are my friends. They won't help you."*

? Huh? What's she talking about?

Being inside the cocoon with Ariadne made me a bit dazed, and I hadn't thought that perhaps my friends on the outside were trying to break through the wall, worried that I might be in danger.

"Back to what we were talking about: Monsters are an essential part of the balancing system for this world. And I just happened to be reborn as one."

*"You just...*happened *to become...a monster?"*

"It was a freak accident. I told you about the passage between our worlds, how sometimes humans from Earth end up reborn here. I don't know what's going on with the reincarnation system on Earth. I was reincarnated in this world with the memories of my past life intact. Maybe something went wrong since I wasn't originally meant for this world. It was just my luck to be reborn as a monster, even though monsters are meant to be simple creatures driven by their instinct to cause harm."

Ariadne's expression clouded over.

"Monsters reproduce without mating, by producing copies of themselves. From the point my soul inhabited a monster's body, it became me, but then

all my offspring were also me. I found the idea of living for an eternity by producing endless copies of myself terrifying, so after Sakura died, I went dormant.

She put her hand to her chest and brightened up with a soft smile. *"But now here I am."*

I shuddered, understanding why she seemed so godlike to me. She'd been alive for a very long time.

"When the head of House Nuir makes a pact with me, our mental bond gets stronger, and their level of ability increases," she went on. *"But as it happens, the pacts I had with the previous Nuir head, and the one before that, brought out more of my predecessor—the monster—instead. I worried that my consciousness would eventually disappear. That's why I'm so glad you called me."*

She reached toward my cheek and stroked it with her soft hand.

I tilted my head to the side. Something wasn't making sense—if I'd awoken her...

"Why did you say we...only have a brief time together?"

"Because your spider already possesses a consciousness!"

Ariadne placed a hand on her belly and stroked it like an excited pregnant lady feeling her stomach, tippy-tapping her spider legs. I guessed that my spider was within her in some embryonic form.

The air around us filled with glittering droplets like a misty rain, followed by a scattering of tiny flowers.

"Wh-whoa!"

So pretty! But...what's going on? Or is this...?

"The birth of...a new soul?"

"Yes! I will finally be released from this monstrous existence!" Ariadne said in a singsong voice, beaming. *"I'll finally be able to die!"*

* * *

Death.

I don't remember how I reacted at that moment.

Our souls had transmigrated once before, so we'd already experienced death.

It's hot. Suffocating. It...hurts? And...it's cold.

I didn't remember the experience very clearly, as I died in an accident. My death was probably almost instantaneous. The memory of my body turning cold was the most vivid of all.

"Say, do you enjoy food?" Ariadne asked me.

"Food? Um... I suppose so... I liked what my...friends would cook for me..."

My mother from my past life had been a homemaker, but her cooking...wasn't particularly good, I guess? Maybe it just didn't suit my tastes; I wasn't sure.

"I also...like the food they give me...where I've been staying."

"You know, I used to love food, too! But the labyrinth spiders' diet is mostly fairies and young women."

I felt the hair on the back of my neck stand on end.

"The first feed my spider mother gave me was some blood that'd spurted from an unlucky adventurer's severed arm."

"Eek!"

"I was scared of my mother and sisters, who preyed on fairies born from pure energy. But what scared me even more was that now that I found blood delicious, I'd start to see the cute fairies as nothing more than delicious morsels...that I might be tempted to devour them."

She still had all her memories from her past life, so that must have made things even more horrific for her. If my previous family had been kind and loving, I might've died from despair in this life.

"I flung myself into an energy stream to end my dreadful existence, but since I happened to possess divinity, I was granted access to the stream. I evolved and gained immortality."

Chance had played a huge role in her life, it seemed.

"What do you mean by... 'divinity'?"

Also... "happened to possess"?

"It's the power from our past world, which is present in everything, like in the air itself. It gets embedded in the personalities and memories we've kept from our past lives. At first, I knew of just three people with that power... Good thing I became the strongest monster in the labyrinth."

She gazed into the distance, lost in her memories.

"Hmm, yes... If I hadn't rescued that baby who'd been thrown into the labyrinth as a sacrifice, I would've given in to despair. And if I hadn't been strong enough to protect her from the other monsters, I'd have ended up slain as a monster myself."

Ariadne waved her fingers, conjuring a soft ball of magic. It wasn't like the magic I knew, though. It had a physical form, and it didn't fade away.

"My taste is different from yours, since I'm a monster, but I've learned to re-create flavors I'd known in my past life with magic."

She offered the ball of magic to me, and I carefully took it from her with both hands. It smelled sweet, like a cake.

"...Shortcake?" I ventured.

"Yep! I based it on the cakes I used to make at the patisserie where I worked in my past life. Try it."

I took a bite.

What a burst of flavor—I tasted slightly tart strawberries, sweet cream,

and sponge cake. With only a few ingredients, each layer of flavor stood out on its own.

"Yummy!" I mumbled with my mouth full, overwhelmed by just how delicious it was.

"Tee-hee. I'm glad you like it. It'll remedy your developmental delay." Ariadne was stroking my head gently, smiling at me, but her gaze was cold. *"You know, ever since I was born into this world, it's been a dream of mine to be reborn here again—as a human this time, so that I can discover the flavors this world's cuisine has to offer. That's why I couldn't be happier to end my existence as a monster, to finally die. Buuut...you know..."*

Her pale fingers tickled my chin, and she continued in a measured, singsong voice that also sounded like an invocation of a curse.

"...I'd like you to tell me something, okay? You've been blessed with the protection of many fairies, and yet you've got this developmental delay. You still have your memories from your past life, but that doesn't explain your extraordinary talents as a fifteen-year-old seamstress.

"I have this special analysis skill, so don't try to hide anything from me, okay?

"...Tell me about the man who plans to marry you—the girl who nurtured her little spider until it was ready to evolve into a divine beast...

"...the girl who will never mature into a woman.

"Tell me about this disgusting creep and his cronies. Tell me about the rotten Royal Palace, so corrupted that it's now a breeding ground for monsters."

She whispered to me that she'd only been vaguely aware of what had been going on around me, since her consciousness had been dormant inside my spider.

I stiffened, mortified.

She's got the completely wrong idea about Argit!

◆

The hideous monsters were turning into black ashes as they cut them down, one after another. They weren't strong, but there were many of them, which made them quite a nuisance.

"Where did these monsters come from?"

"We must not forget that the Founder's partner beast originated as a spider from the labyrinth," the elderly butler said. Everybody gasped.

"Are you saying the divine beast is creating them…?"

"Welus, do you think Yui is safe?"

"Lady Yui is perfectly fine at the moment, Your Highness." Mimachi answered Argit's question before the butler had the chance as she swiftly stabbed and slashed the attacking spider monsters. "My bond with her hasn't been severed, and I don't sense fear or desperation from her."

"Thank goodness."

"But why was she taken from us?" Amnart asked, cocking his head.

Hania touched her lips with her fingers, also puzzled by this.

"Was it because…she spoke the divine beast's name?"

"Perhaps it was only legible to those deserving to see her," Welus suggested.

"I can see that being the case!" said Mimachi, nodding eagerly. "Like, your magic needs to be this powerful to read the sacred name."

Mimachi went around the wall of the cocoon, looking for a way in. She did find an opening and went inside. She came back out after a few minutes.

"You know, I had a bad feeling when you mentioned a labyrinth earlier."

"Ah. Is it bigger inside than it is outside?"

"You've been suspecting that much, huh? Yeah, it is a labyrinth, complete with monsters. They're too much for me to handle, and there's no sneaking past them, even with my stealth skills."

"Let's assess our strength. Thankfully, the civil officials didn't get trapped here with us. Yet even we are lacking in weapons, and neither did we bring any medicine."

"Hania is the only one without any weapons, I think?"

"You're wrong, Am," she replied, hoisting up the skirt of her dress to reveal small bags attached to her garter belts. She detached them and took out two brass knuckles and a pair of gloves. "They're an engagement present from my brother. He was concerned that someone might try to attack me following the announcement of our engagement; that's why he gave me these so that I could deal with such trouble by myself, without inconveniencing you."

"That Ian…"

Hania put on the gloves, and the knuckles over them. She bumped her fists together, and flames appeared around her hands.

"Oh, the effect is weaker than before…? Is it because fairies don't want to make an enemy of the divine beast?"

Amnart sighed. "A fairy weapon is a bit too much for an engagement gift, I'd say…"

"Yeah, I don't think we can count on the fairies to help us in this fight, but at least your fairy familiar should help protect you, Lady Hania."

"My armor fairy doesn't seem too keen on this, either," Stolle added, stroking her armor, the gauntlets, and the cuirass, feeling their power drop.

The only reason she didn't seem particularly alarmed was that owing to the pledge that bound her to Yui as her protector, she could sense at all times whether Yui was in any danger. Nonetheless, she cursed herself for not being strong enough yet, for being so reliant on the fairies' support.

"I've read that the labyrinth keeper has the ability to both create monsters and expand space, but it's different knowing something and experiencing it," Stolle said, picking up a magic stone dropped by a monster she'd just slain as they made their way through the labyrinth.

"According to a folktale, the castle—the Royal Palace—was built on top of a labyrinth." Hania knocked on one of the walls, listening for the sound it made.

"I'd say there's a high chance that particular folktale is a retelling of a historical event," Amnart agreed. "The tales about how the Founder, the original spider, and the first king met, though—those are all pure fancy."

"The Founder was saved by her dad, right?"

"Hmm, Toluamia showed good judgment enclosing us in that magic circle. If it weren't for that, perhaps the entire palace would have been overtaken by this labyrinth."

As a rule, labyrinths were infested with monsters. Slaying all of them only brought a brief respite before they respawned.

"Now, that'd be a hassle, with all those sitting ducks," Mimachi said slowly.

She didn't mean to mock the palace officials for their inability to fight—she was actually deeply relieved that these valuable yet very vulnerable people wouldn't be put at risk.

Mimachi took stock of their team.

They had the elderly butler, who seemed to be a jack-of-all-trades.

Next, the captain of the royal guards, an expert in defense.

The battle maid, a trained assassin and a capable scout.

The powered-up armored maiden with well-balanced offensive and defensive skills.

The former-king-turned-adventurer, freed from crimes of fashion and now dressed in top-notch blessed garments, armed with a freezing magic sword, turning his foes into icicles that were child's play to shatter… (Wasn't that a labyrinth sword? Where did he get that? He didn't have it three days ago.)

Then there was the queen-to-be, an expert martial artist armed with fiery brass knuckles, who wanted to be the vanguard. (But of course, Mimachi wouldn't let her—she was too precious!)

Finally, the king, a first-rate swordmaster and martial artist, perfect for a support role owing to his ability to use plant-fairy magic to tie up foes with vines. (Mimachi wasn't going to allow him to engage in combat, either. You don't risk the king!)

"We don't seem to have anyone specialized in ranged combat, but given the structure of this labyrinth, it wouldn't offer us much of an advantage anyway," Welus commented.

"What could be the divine beast's objective, I wonder?" Argit asked anxiously, worried about Yui.

Stolle was about to say something, but in the end, she pursed her lips. She had a feeling that this divine beast was similar to Mimachi, but it was just her gut feeling, and she didn't want to unnecessarily worry anyone with her guess.

"Lady Yui is actually well-equipped to deal with perverts," she muttered to herself.

◆

A part of the wall became reflective like a mirror, and then Argit and his companions were displayed on it like on a TV. Ariadne noticed with surprise that I began panicking, unsure if I'd be able to properly explain in order to clear up her misunderstanding of Argit's motivations. Instead, she asked me for permission to see my memories for herself. A thread of magic connected my forehead to hers.

She seemed a bit disappointed when I readily agreed to let her peer into my mind. I wasn't bothered by her reading my memories because she said she'd only be able to see the ones from this life, not the past one, with the exception of the past-life events I'd been reminiscing about since my rebirth. I didn't want her to see me when I was depressed and had no skills to speak of, or when I was still trying to live up to my past-life parents' twisted expectations. Those were dark times.

"Oh, I understand now…," she said, frowning deeply.

I cocked my head. *"Um, Ariadne…?"*

"Call me Aria," she replied, twiddling her fingers.

I saw on the screen that a wall had suddenly appeared in front of Argit and his party, blocking their path.

"I made it so there's only one way they can go now."

I looked at her, not quite understanding what was going on. She smiled uncomfortably, weaving her fingers through the air some more.

"I can't change the size of the labyrinth at this point or erase the pseudoboss."

The image on the screen changed, as if she'd switched to a different channel. Now it was showing a woman.

"This is the source of the miasma. It's her curse."

The woman was exuding tar-black smoke. There was something rotten about it; just looking at it made me feel sick. The woman's body seemed to be made of the same black substance.

It was like something out of a horror movie. She was swaying left and right, then she abruptly turned her head so that we saw her directly.

Her eye sockets were empty.

"Eeeek!" I screamed at the chilling sight.

"She's a wraith… They're highly intelligent."

"N-no—stop it! You're scaring me!"

"Oh? You're not a fan of horror stuff?"

This shouldn't have rattled me so much, but I couldn't stop shaking.

?

"Wait…" It wasn't fear that was making me shake. *"I'm…grossed out, not scared. The energy she's directing at me…is making me feel like…I walked into a kitchen…swarming with vermin."*

"Ahhh, that makes sense."

As a side note, I said "vermin" because I couldn't stand hearing the name of those bugs out loud…and out of consideration for a friend from my past life, I never said the word out loud, either. I could handle one of those bugs at a time, but a whole group of them… Ew! Although, even a single one of them could be just as bad if it came at me, in which case I'd scream in sheer terror.

"The best part about being reborn in this world is that you won't find any of those black demons lurking in kitchens," Aria said in a completely serious voice.

So they didn't exist in this world. I didn't know, never having been in a kitchen in either of the two households where I'd lived. Somehow, it was still a relief to hear I had exactly zero chances of ever seeing one here.

"Thank goodness!" I said.

Aria patted my head.

"In any case, she must be defeated, or the door to this chamber won't open… I hope your friends can take care of this remnant of the curse at least. You've

already got a lot on your plate, with people expecting you to lift the curse, which has nothing to do with you."

Huh?

"Is this wraith...based on the woman...who cursed the Realm Weaveguardian?" I asked.

A smile returned to Aria's face.

"Ah, the Realm Weaveguardian... Me and Sakura's masterpiece. She's like our child. We designed this country so that fairies would be safe and happy here. Humans were just an afterthought to us."

Again, I noticed that Aria's smile didn't reach as far as her eyes. Was she upset with me for having boldly claimed I could cure the tapestry fairy? No, she was mad about something that'd taken place much earlier—humans allowing one of their rotten brethren near the fairy in the first place.

*"Cuteness is a lovable quality. How could a human blessed with the gift to see the cute fairies wish harm upon them? The king should've destroyed that filthy human's homeland without mercy. **The royals have lost sight of their priorities.**"*

That's...a radical view.

Aria was in many ways like a goddess, but of the *kishibojin* type, the mother of devils.

While we were chatting, Argit and his party reached the pseudoboss. He called out to her, and her expression changed. Her lips curled into a smile; she seemed thrilled to see him...although that only made her look more grotesque.

Ugh, I can't stand this. I just want to go back to my needlework.

"I hate yandere types. I hope they torture her to death, giving the original some nasty nightmares," Aria said, propping her chin with her hand.

Aha. So the wraith is connected to the former queen?

My gaze drifted from the golden thread filling the chamber to Aria, her upper body covered only with her long hair, and I was suddenly overcome with an uncontrollable desire.

The golden threads were formed from condensed energy. Magic, perhaps? Whatever it was, it certainly belonged to Aria.

"Would you...mind if I used this...to make clothes for you?" I asked.

Aria was thrown by my question, and she dialed down her air of seduction, making big eyes at me. Then she smiled.

"You're an artisan, aren't you?" She gently stroked my hair. *"I'm glad you're the first otherworlder I got to chat with after my long slumber."*

I felt the same. I was so happy to have met Aria.

I didn't have the tools of my trade with me, having left my sewing and knitting needles with Stolle. I made a mental note to procure a dressmaking kit I could carry with me at all times. Fortunately, the golden thread was a strange kind of material, both physical and ethereal at the same time, and I found that I could work it with tools made from my own magic.

In a way, the golden threads were a crystallization of Aria's concentrated magic, I supposed. But unlike my own magic, which I could shape into needles and such for use with magical threads, Aria's golden threads existed in the physical realm, too.

Wait—isn't this...?

Yes!

The missing material for repairing the tapestry! Threads made from ultra-condensed magic—they were used in Stolle's armor, too. My spider's level had been too low to produce anything like this before. But was this all?

"Can I heal the Realm Weaveguardian...with this?"

"Her cursed arm needs to be cut off, so you'll also need the power of a high-level wind fairy."

Cut off?

I was so focused on healing her that this option didn't occur to me at all. So gloves wouldn't do the trick. Her arm had to be removed and remade. At the same time, I would have to cut out the damaged parts of the tapestry, reweaving them, connecting the threads. I'd be working in parallel, just as I did when embroidering Hania's dress. Of course, this would be far more difficult, but I was prepared for that.

"You'll need to destroy the severed arm with magic from a high-level flame fairy... Ah, you know one already, don't you?"

"Lady Hania's fairy?"

"She has a bond with a high-level harvest fairy, so I'm sure she can summon flames of purification."

Ah, so it wasn't only plant fairies whose color was green. And the size of fairies indicated their level, with the human-sized ones being the most powerful? I hadn't seen many of those...

I also realized that I didn't know how to recognize wind fairies.

"What color...are the wind fairies?"

"Never seen one before, huh?" Aria pointed up. *"That's because they're transparent."*

Well, that explains it.

"You might be able to spot some in strong gusts of wind. They'll look like they're made of glass. Fairies of mixed alignment who have strong wind affinity are visible, though."

I'd hardly ever been outdoors in my current life, and even when I traveled to the town near Rodin's residence, I did so in a carriage. I had felt gentle breezes on my cheeks, but never a strong gust of wind.

All fairies were slightly see-through to begin with, but now that I thought about it, I remembered a fairy who had been more transparent than the others. Were they part wind fairy?

"You can also use a wind-property magic sword from the labyrinth. That might be easier to find."

Hmmm, I think I'm out of my depth here.

In the pseudoboss room, Argit and company had managed to behead the wraith. All of a sudden, the room filled with black hair.

176

•••CHAPTER 8•••

Battle

The room was empty but for a dark human shadow. Argit gasped in horror.

"Lestlana?"

Even though she was a tar-black wraith, he recognized her by her shape and the expression on her face.

"I see now… The miasma has come from her curse," Welus said.

Mimachi hit her palm with her fist. "Right! When Lady Yui teased out some of the wicked energy that sickened the Realm Weaveguardian, it turned into this!"

Amnart sighed. "What has everything come to…? Monsters are being bred at the palace, which ought to be a sanctum blessed by the Realm Weaveguardian…"

"Urgh… And this one is made in the old queen's image."

"Oh? Is this really what Queen Lestlana looks like? I heard she was a great beauty, but she seems so…hideous to me, even for a specter," commented Hania, peering curiously at the wraith.

She was the only one in this group who had not seen the queen. She wondered if the wraith seemed even more repulsive to her because she was so prejudiced against the old queen, detesting her for wishing harm onto Amnart.

"When she showed up here, she was just an apathetic, harmless woman," Mimachi remarked.

"Yes, I remember that..." Stolle nodded. "She arrived together with her lady-in-waiting, whose character was far from noble. If at least her lady-in-waiting had been a decent person, a sole ally to the queen through her life full of abuse, perhaps she wouldn't have turned out like this. By the time she arrived in our kingdom for the marriage, it was too late to save her."

As she spoke, Stolle reached for the hilt of her spear. It was just a hilt, without a blade attached, but Yui had told Stolle how to activate the power of her legendary armor to complete the weapon... A flame shot out from the hilt, taking the form of a spear.

Stolle leaped up to the ceiling, taking aim at the monster standing stupidly in the middle of the room with a macabre smile.

"Hyaaah!"

The wraith looked up just as Stolle landed, planting her boots on the monster's chest and cutting off her head in one swift slash. The head fell on the floor...but then the creature's dark hair began to slither around like snakes, spreading out through the room.

"Ngh... Kweh!" The knight got slammed into the wall by a writhing tangle of hair. Choking for air, he waved his sword around to free himself.

Stolle charged again at the headless body of the wraith, piercing it with her fire spear. It turned to ashes with a rather comical *poof*!

"Oh?"

"Stolle! The head!"

The mass of hair lifted the severed head.

*   *   *

"M-my...daaarling...Aaargiiit!"

She let out a nauseatingly sweet screech. There was no mistaking it: That was the voice of Argit's second wife, the former queen Lestlana.

The mass of hair was shakily holding up the talking head, but some of the tangles now reached out for Argit. He was able to fend them off with his ice sword, but this was not the right element to use against this foe. The frozen hairs would shatter into more pieces, which would then start creeping toward him, too.

"Your Highness!" Stolle called out to him. She was growing tired from chasing the head around.

"Don't worry about me! I don't have the right weapon, but you can destroy the head!"

"Aye!"

"Watch out, Stolle!" Mimachi cut through a bunch of hair that'd been trying to wrap itself around Stolle. As she hopped over the hair, landing in a squat and supporting herself with one hand on the ground, she noticed something. "We can get help from the fairies again!"

She discharged her magic into the spot on the floor she was touching.

"Please lend me your power!"

Several pillars appeared in the room, arranged like log steps at a playground.

"Stolle!"

"Got it!"

Stolle jumped onto them to get closer to the head she had been following around the room, but the head kept dipping under the waves of hair, disappearing out of sight just as she thought she'd gotten within reach.

"Cutting them only creates more... What else can we do?"

181

Suddenly, a golden flame appeared in one corner of the room.

"Your Highness! This way! It's you she's targeting!"

"Welus, I have to protect Amnart. His safety is more important than mine!"

"Your Highness, we have to use you as a lure! It's our only chance!" Hania slammed her fist into the ground, and another golden flame shot up. A bunch of writhing hair that had been chasing her stopped and flinched away from the fire, as if in fear.

In this way, Hania cleared the hair off one corner of the room, creating a safe space for the old butler and Amnart. She forged a path through the hair to the royal guard and freed him from the binding tangles.

"I imagine it's difficult for you to stand by watching, leaving Lady Hania and Lady Stolle to do most of the fighting," the old butler said to Amnart.

"Maybe I'm not so powerless after all..."

A thought occurred to Amnart while he was following the guardian fairies with his eyes. The flame-red rose on his chest...

Amnart traced down his cloak with his fingertips until he touched the embroidered flower made from the combined magic of his and Hania's fairy. He charged it with his magic, and the flower appeared in his hand in its original form again, except that now it was burning with fiery magic.

"Oh! This is amazing—I can use the power of fire!"

Amnart gasped, mesmerized by the flame, which did not burn him. Until then, the only powers he'd had were those of his own fairy, and they were all related to making plants grow.

He wouldn't have been able to use this power without a suitable medium, and the rose Yui had made for him from the power of the two fairies was simply ideal.

A thicket of burning, thorny roses surrounded Amnart.

"Oh?"

He looked around, confused. He hadn't yet tried to wield the power of the flame rose...

His butler smiled wryly at him.

"Your Majesty, this is the effect of the crown."

"Are you saying this is the guardian skill of my fairy, whose power is to look after the land in our kingdom?" He'd heard about it but had never experienced it before.

"Amnart! Can you create more of those shrubs?!" Argit shouted, surprising his son with this suggestion.

Amnart reached his hand toward Hania, who was dragging back the knight she'd saved from being choked by the writhing hair.

"Hania, will you help me?"

Welus, the butler, jumped over the fiery rose hedge and hoisted the knight over his shoulder, freeing up Hania.

"Lady Hania, please go to His Majesty."

"Thank you! I will!"

The burning roses parted, making way for Hania. Once inside their circle, she took Amnart's hand...and the roses spread throughout the room, growing into another thick hedge around Argit.

"Aaaaaarrrrr—"

Surrounded by flaming flowers on all sides, the tangles of hair began to burn. From her high vantage point on one of the pillars, Stolle finally spotted the wraith's head, which was moving in Argit's direction. It had transformed, the mouth now full of sharklike teeth, the hair morphed into insect-like legs upon which it scurried on the floor, trailing goopy drool. Argit was struck with terror—anyone would be if they had such a monster rushing toward them.

"Stolle!"

"I've got this!"

Argit struck the monstrosity away with his sword, and Stolle pounced on it, piercing it with her flame spear.

"—giiiit... Wh...whyyyyy?"

◆

The wall separating me from Argit and his party flashed and disappeared. They saw me and made as if to run toward me, but Aria's cold stare froze them in place.

"I wouldn't give them a passing grade...," she started in Japanese, but then she corrected herself, switching to the language spoken in this kingdom. "You're too weak. How are you hoping to heal her?"

Aria extended her hand, and the Realm Weaveguardian appeared beside her, placing her healthy hand in Aria's. Her lacy dress rustled pleasantly.

Aria began to explain that she'd created the wraith out of the fragment of the curse I had removed from the Divine Fairy Cloth, the Realm Weaveguardian. Meanwhile, I started making a new glove for the fairy, using Aria's golden thread this time.

Pouring magic into this thread made it strong but elastic. It emitted a beautiful sound when I moved it. Without magic, it would stick to other threads, which could have a use when weaving fabric, but it was the last thing I needed when making lace. I screamed internally when the threads stuck together at first.

As Aria and Argit talked at length, I only half listened, working the lace in a pattern I'd learned. I also added a motif based on the purifying magic

184

circle I saw on the tapestry. Aria was providing me with thread, but she offered no guidance, so I had to rely on my memory alone.

I pictured the pattern I was following in my head, keeping track of when to infuse the thread with magic and when to leave it "empty," allowing it to stick.

The fairy's cursed arm would eventually have to be cut off, and then it would certainly turn into a monster, even without Aria's involvement. If even the vestiges of the curse I'd managed to remove had turned into that horrifying wraith, the entire arm would become something comparable to the final boss in a video game. That's why I wanted to gradually dampen the curse's power, before that happened…

Well, I should be more honest here. My primary motivation was the desire to practice my needlework techniques! Until that point, I would either sew with magic or without. Switching between the two was new to me, but I was working as fast as before…which was the problem. It was like muscle memory, my hands following the movements required to work the pattern, too fast for my brain to catch up and switch the magic on and off.

Oh no! I was sure I'd make a mistake sooner or later…

At the same time, I was too anxious to take my time and go slow. I had to complete the glove before the curse sensed what was afoot and crept up the threads.

Aria's golden thread stayed in place. From the look of it, it would only dissolve after a few weeks of lessening the curse with purification magic. Which was good.

The first glove I'd made for the fairy could only scatter some of the curse's power, but it was bound to return. Aria had gathered it and formed it into a monster, which we could defeat, making this part of the curse go away for good. If it weren't for that, that first glove would have had no effect at all.

My spirits sank as I thought about it. I chided myself for having had too much confidence in the healing power of my blessweaving.

"Nobody noticed at the time that the curse had been scattered rather than healed. But it did bring some relief to the Realm Weaveguardian."

That's what Aria had said, at least. Scattering the curse, having it transform into monsters, and then defeating them—this wasn't an efficient way to deal with it, and it carried a high risk.

You can choose to persist with a difficult, inefficient solution, hoping it will work better as you get more practiced at it. Or you can invent a new, better one.

Being able to sew faster than a sewing machine, imbuing clothes with mysterious effects, wasn't the pinnacle of achievement. It wasn't the solution to all problems.

I became so engrossed in what I was doing that I completely stopped listening to the conversation taking place around me. I heard people talking, but the words didn't register in my head.

Unbeknownst to me, Aria was telling Argit that her consciousness would last at most another year. That it would take several years for my spider to grow as powerful as she was. That the Realm Weaveguardian's arm had to be cut off, and that this could only be done with the help of a high-level wind fairy or with a magic sword with the severance effect. That the arm of the fairy would automatically turn into a monster once it was separated from her body.

She was relaying to them what she had already told me before the wall between our chamber and the boss room disappeared, although there were a few items she left out. Such as the fact that there was very high likelihood of her being reborn in this world again, quite possibly as my daughter, since we shared a special bond given that we'd both transmigrated from Earth.

Nobody questioned why Aria and I spoke an unfamiliar foreign language.

"Don't worry about that. They'll just assume it's a special language that

only those who have special powers, or are worthy, can understand. If they ask you about it, just look at them as if you don't really get how it works yourself, and they'll come up with some plausible explanation by themselves."

"So the wedding will take place in six months?"

Hmm?

Aria's words caught my attention just as I finally finished the lace I'd been struggling with so much. I had no idea what they were talking about.

"A…wedding? In—six months?"

I gave them a blank look, wondering whose wedding this was about.

"King Amnart and Lady Hania's, as well as yours and Lord Argit's." Mimachi filled me in, suddenly appearing behind me.

"It'd be best if you found the fairy or the sword needed to cut the cursed arm off in time for the wedding." Aria sighed. "The woman who put the curse on the Realm Weaveguardian has likely lost her mind to the point where her jealousy can be triggered by anything related to the royal family. Even if it were only King Amnart getting married, that would be enough for the curse to become uncontrollable. But at the same time, that will make it easier to separate it from the Weaveguardian." She stroked the fairy's back tenderly. "In any case, you have a year at most to accomplish this. Also, keep in mind that I can only be awoken twice at most within that time."

Aria eyed me and the fairy affectionately, but when she turned to Argit and the others, her gaze turned steely.

"I only have enough power left to protect Yui and the Realm Weaveguardian."

You have six months to become strong; otherwise, be prepared to die.

* * *

Her voice echoed in the heads of Argit and his companions.

◆

Having finished the difficult part of the glove for the fairy, I snapped out of that state of hyperfocus. By the time I tied off the thread, Aria was mostly done talking to my friends.

Argit was rubbing his temples, muttering to himself, "Perverted old man fancying little girls…?" evidently in deep shock. I guessed that Aria explained to him why she'd snatched me away from him at the first opportunity.

The others also seemed shaken.

"So it'd be ten times stronger? Ha-ha… We're gonna die…"

"Hmm. It would seem you have not been trained properly. You must never whine in front of your mistress."

"Owww! Welus, let gooo! You're crushing my head!"

It was usually Stolle or the housekeeper bringing Mimachi in line, but this time, she'd fallen prey to the butler (?), Welus, who'd picked her up by her head and was holding her up high, with her feet dangling in the air.

Their antics somehow made everyone a bit more at ease, relieving the tension in the room. Well, to be precise, Welus had never lost his composure to begin with, and I couldn't be sure about Stolle, since she wore a closed helmet.

"Well then, I'll be going back to sleep soon," Aria said when I finished making the glove, producing a pink ribbon out of somewhere and tying it on the fairy's arm at the edge of the curse.

The ribbon was a beautiful cherry-blossom pink, with a golden gloss. It

immediately occurred to me that it must have been the work of Aria's partner, Sakura. It was made of exquisitely fine lace.

I sensed there was something different about it. It had a similar aura to items inhabited by fairies, but it wasn't that. Aria noticed that I was trying to puzzle that out.

"It's a lucky item. You see, in this world, there's a random chance of craft objects gaining divine powers. It's a bit like the treasure appearing in the labyrinth. Although, these objects must be extremely well-crafted for a chance of this happening, and there's no guarantee that even the finest masterpiece will gain this power. Also, you cannot predict what this power will be."

"Huh?!"

Suddenly, I really wanted to become the creator of such an object.

"It's an amulet to ward off evil. I will soon die, but she will live on, as long as this country exists," Aria whispered to me in Japanese with a smile.

To us artisans, our creations are like our children—we can't help thinking of them with affection. The Realm Weaveguardian was not only a beautiful work of craft, but a fairy, a sentient being. Of course Aria loved her deeply and thought of her as the child born to her and Sakura.

"This ribbon was my prized treasure. Now she'll have a memento to remember me by."

Aria sounded so incredibly sad. The Realm Weaveguardian also looked at her sorrowfully, reluctant to part. The two embraced for a moment.

I made a resolution when I saw that look of love and loneliness in their eyes: to find a way to keep the Realm Weaveguardian safe even if the country were to fall into ruin.

The Nuir family had gone to the dogs. The royals were upstanding people right now, but there was no guarantee that trend would continue into the future. A threat might come from the outside, against their intentions, as in the case of Argit and his ex-wife.

*   *   *

That day, my bucket list considerably expanded.

"Ah, you must also know that one of my clones has fully reverted to a monster. The other has been tainted already as well, so you must restrain both the spider and its owner with Collars of Servitude."

"These two clones…are still in the hands of the Nuir family?"

I felt embarrassed to hear that, but it wasn't much of a surprise. With how things were at my family home, I had a feeling that might've been the case.

"It's that man and his daughter, huh…?" Even the gentle Amnart became stone-faced for a moment.

My sister's insulting behavior toward Hania had in fact outraged the king. *She's finished*, I thought.

"How come there have been no reports of monster attacks if they're keeping one?"

"The servants at their house are as rotten as the Nuirs. Let's keep an eye on them, and as soon as we find any proof of a monster attack, we enter their residence and slay it. It will be good practice before our battle with the curse of Lestlana," Argit proposed with a chilling smile.

"Just make sure you do kill it," Aria said softly as she withdrew into her shiny cocoon, making herself cozy for her next long nap. She didn't seem to have much sympathy for her clones.

The cocoon closed over Aria. The walls and ceiling of the labyrinth flashed golden and began to disappear. Somehow, the light didn't dazzle us. I noticed many small creatures…leftover monsters. They scurried toward the light, creaking and squeaking, and then they, too, vanished.

It felt like we were moving even though the space around us remained motionless, and I grew a little nauseous. I didn't notice anything like this when Aria was morphing the space around us to create the labyrinth.

The walls nearest to the cocoon faded away first as the labyrinth kept shrinking. At last, its outer wall vanished, and we found ourselves in the middle of the magic circle drawn by the magician with the staff.

"Your Majesty! Are you unharmed?!"

The magician fell to his knees. I could tell from his sickly appearance that he'd used up all his magic.

"Yes, I'm perfectly fine. I'm sorry I made you worry, Toluamia," Amnart replied, crouching to pick up the magic stones piled up at his feet. "That was a lot of monsters. You'd scarcely believe this is a royal palace..."

People were talking over one another, as those who had been anxiously waiting outside the magic circle wanted to hear what had happened to us. I ignored the din, watching the cocoon get smaller and smaller. It turned glossy and hard, resembling an egg. When it stopped shrinking, it was larger than a chicken egg. Maybe half the size of an ostrich egg. In any case, it was bigger than my spider used to be—I could picture it comfortably nestling inside a chicken egg.

Then I heard something...

Crrrack!

The shell opened, and white hands poked out of it.

"?!"

The creature stuck out its arms and then pushed out its head between them. It exhaled loudly.

"Are you...a fairy?"

It did look somewhat like a fairy. Its face bore a resemblance both to Aria and to me. The creature tilted its head to the side sleepily, reaching its arms toward me. It wanted me to hold it.

I cupped my hands, and the creature jumped down from the egg. As I suspected, its lower body was that of a spider.

My spider...

She was tiny, but she was now a divine beast like Aria.

◆

There was a lot to talk about afterward, but apparently, I was so tired, I slept through most of it.

I was stroking my "transformed"...freshly hatched (?) spider when Argit came over to check in on me.

"How did it go?" he asked.

I turned around and showed him the cute fairylike creature in my hands. He looked like he wanted to say something nice about her but just couldn't manage it... His smile was strained, plastered on.

I was grinning, then suddenly collapsed. I'd only fallen asleep from exhaustion, but at first...

"Blood drained out of everyone's faces in, like, an instant."

"They even stopped breathing."

"It should've been obvious that you were just so tired. Personally, I was surprised you lasted that long."

I had to apologize to Mimachi and Stolle. After I passed out from exhaustion, they had to take care of me and carry me to a bed.

Mimachi was right—considering all I'd done that day, or to be precise, all I'd done within only half a day, it beggared belief that I hadn't run out of energy much earlier. I'd scattered some of the Realm Weaveguardian's curse, woven blessings into Hania's dress while blending the magic from both her and Amnart's fairy, then made a dress for Aria and another glove for the Realm Weaveguardian to seal the curse. Ah, and I also made a formal suit for Amnart. I supposed I owed it to Aria's healing magic that I found enough stamina for all that.

I woke up in the doctor's office at Rodin's home. At my bedside was the doctor who Rodin had hired to look after me. He was in tears.

Rodin had me undergo a detailed medical examination following my encounter with the Founder's spider—Aria—which included a brief stay in a monster-ridden labyrinth. He chose the same doctor who'd cared for me before, when I was nearly starved to death.

As for the results of the examination...

Even with the fairies' protection, the abuse I'd suffered over so many years had left my body in a severely weakened state. When the doctor first met me, he estimated that I wouldn't even live to age thirty, and I was highly unlikely to be able to have children. But since my return to the labyrinth, my condition had significantly improved...

While my physical development would keep progressing at a very slow pace and my appearance was unlikely to change very much, it seemed very likely that I would be able to bear children. The doctor's words were welcomed with tears of joy by the maids.

I guessed it was the effect of Aria's cake. Her healing magic continued its regenerative work on my body over the next three days as well, making me very drowsy. I was too sleepy to rejoice at my recovery together with the maids. I felt as if I was walking in a dream.

Besides, honestly, all I wanted from life was to be a seamstress until the end. I wasn't rattled at all when they told me that initially it seemed I wouldn't live to my thirtieth birthday, maybe because I had memories of my past life. Mentally, I was in my thirties already. Having seen Aria—a second-lifer like me—getting excited about being able to die soon might also have played a part in desensitizing me to the idea. Or maybe this new information needed more time to sink in.

I was relieved that I'd be able to have children, since there was a high chance that Aria would be reborn as either my child or grandchild.

I'd have to do something about the Nuir heritage. Aria had been a chef in her past life. I didn't want to force her to become a seamstress in the next if she wasn't interested in that.

The Nuirs' pact with the spiders was in Aria's name, so it was only valid until her death. Afterward, I would be able to name my spider and forge a new pact. I wanted to make it so that the spiders wouldn't be automatically inherited by my descendants, but instead, they would be able to choose their human partners based on merit of both character and sewing ability.

Both in my previous life and this one, romance was of no interest to me, so the idea of having a child one day was very abstract to me. I was to become Aria's mother? I did want that, but I couldn't imagine myself as a mother.

Hmm... I could make adorable bootees for my baby. And clothes... Thinking about all the cute little things I could make for my future child woke me up, and I realized I would likely get hooked on making soft toys.

In commoner households, generally the mother would be responsible for making clothes for her family. There were clothes stores in towns and cities, but most of them sold secondhand clothes, while the rest catered to nobility and other wealthy customers.

Clothes stores also sold fabric. The stores frequented by commoners bought and sold fabric scraps so cheaply, they were often used as stuffing for cushions. Those cushions were rather hard and heavy, like Japanese *zabuton* floor cushions. Cotton existed in this world, so you'd think cotton wool would make a better choice, but fabric scraps were readily available, and they didn't have any other use. Maybe except in mending clothes? Patchwork wasn't a technique known in this world.

There were dolls, but they were expensive. My parents had bought one for my sister. They were made of porcelain, like bisque dolls from my previous world, but I thought their features were pretty creepy. I could easily imagine one coming to life at night and trying to kill people. My sister showed me her new doll, trying to make me jealous, but I only felt terrified. Of the doll and my sister's lack of aesthetic sense. It also terrified me to think that there were many highborn girls who desired those horrific dolls.

As for stuffed toys... There were some, but they were rather...flat. Like little pillows in animal shapes. They were cute, I admit, but having grown up in a world with a great variety of stuffed toys, I felt they were disappointingly basic.

I thought I'd try my hand at making items this world had not seen before. First, I made a patchwork cushion. Next, a handbag and a drawstring bag. Moving on in size, I made a patchwork quilt.

Then I made a cute chibi-style doll and a hand puppet with a moving mouth. I got into stuffed toys next, beginning with the classic teddy before all sorts of other animals. I made *amigurumi*, too.

I was to move soon, so everyone around me was busy with preparations, and there I was, increasing the number of my belongings that would have to be packed and transported. Ah, I nearly forgot to mention that the date of my transfer to Argit's residence had been moved up, on account of the boss-battle marriage being in half a year's time. I'd have to make wedding outfits suitable for fighting monsters.

Once I was no longer sleepy all day long, I felt strong and well, but the maids wouldn't let me help with anything, even though they had their hands full. That's why I spent my time making cute little things. The household fairies took a keen interest in them.

Fairies could pass through people if they wanted to, although they rarely did that. One day, I was entertaining one of the maids with the hand

puppet (which proved to be a huge hit), making roaring noises, when a fairy stuck their head out of the puppet's mouth. They looked as if they were wearing an animal onesie.

"A-adorable…!" I gasped with admiration, greatly confusing the maid.

Another day, once life returned to normal after the recent adventures featuring monster slaying and royal-engagement announcements, I donated the soft toys I'd made to an orphanage. Some of the children asked me to teach them how to make toys like that, which I did. Consequently, plushies made by the orphans became a source of income for the institution, and there were quite a few children who decided they wanted to become seamstresses.

◆

"Lady Yui has three fairy companions who never leave her side. One is of tree affinity, another of the moontide, and the last one of darkness. With her pale skin and silver hair, I surmise her body might be weak to heat," Skur said.

Mimachi nodded. "She's really compatible with His Highness!"

"Yes, I also do not bear heat very well. Also, only two of the known mazes may yield wind weapons." Argit marked two locations on the map with pins.

"A trip to the mountain peak will be too strenuous for Lady Yui." Endelia removed one of the pins.

"If I may… As a medically trained maid, I would like to recommend somewhere with hot springs for Lady Yui's health. Should her moontide guardian fairy decide to desert, I'll be right there to look after Lady Yui."

"Hey! Hot springs are like home to us Terra!"

"I would, of course, ensure Mimachi stays well away from Lady Yui during her bath."

"?!"

"Why do you look so disappointed, pervert?" Stolle grabbed Mimachi by the back of her head and lifted her into the air, but the maid pouted without any sign of remorse. She whistled.

"~♪ ~~~♪ ~~♪"

"So good at whistling, aren't you?" Ulde smiled, pinching Mimachi's cheeks to make her stop.

"Well, this is the better of the two choices anyway. It's within the territory of House Menes, which is one of the locations I was considering for my retirement," Argit said conclusively.

"If you could find us a hidden cottage near the labyrinth, where Lady Yui could stay while I kept watch over her health...," the doctor-maid requested, bowing her head low.

Argit, Rodin, Stolle, Mimachi, Rodin's housekeeper, Ulde, Skur, and a chosen few stood around a table on which a map of the kingdom was spread out.

"Rodin, I hope you don't mind me taking your housekeeper with us on this trip."

"Urgh!"

"Mimachi, you need to be reeducated."

"N-n-no! Lady Endelia, have mercy on meee!"

The housekeeper glared at Mimachi, who was still dangling in Stolle's viselike grip, her cheeks looking red and a little puffy. Rodin ignored the maids' altercation, smiling hesitantly at Argit.

"Of course, Your Highness. I have Ulde, and Skur can help as needed."

"You only employ the most talented people, don't you?"

After dropping Mimachi like a bag of trash, Stolle turned toward Rodin and nodded. Then she touched her fingertips to her chin.

"There's one more thing…"

"I have already notified all guilds that I'm looking to hire a swordmaster who wields a sword of separation."

Lying on the ground, Mimachi took the opportunity to try to peek under a maid's dress…but she was suddenly enveloped in darkness summoned by the housekeeper's fairy.

"I also let them know we're looking for someone with a wind-affinity guardian fairy."

The housekeeper petted her fairy.

"They might be unwilling to take up such a job offer, though. Wind fairies are fond of footloose, fancy-free people," she remarked.

"I…may know someone who fits the bill, but they don't seem all that much in tune with their fairy," Argit said, looking into the distance with a sigh. The person he was thinking of was someone he'd had to deal with before Yui made him his first proper clothes.

"Ah… I think I know who you mean. Should I get in touch? Offering not money, but a garment made by Lady Yui as payment?"

"Only if they're in the Labyrinth Guild."

"I must apologize to you, Linne. I'll be taking your seamstress away from you."

"Lord Rodin, you owe me no apologies. Lady Yui is simply outstanding. She has done so much sewing for the household that I'll have difficulty finding anything to do for the next seamstress you hire, even factoring in the time I'll have to spend showing her the ropes."

*　　*　　*

Argit shut his eyes. Then he slowly opened them again. There was a glint of excitement in his amber eyes.

"I hereby ask you to lend me your help in my final mission as a former king of this land."

Everyone stood up straighter, nodding solemnly.

Afterword

Hello!

It's been a few years since someone suggested that I publish *Maiden of the Needle*...

I'm Zeroki, the slow-paced author!

I bragged to my younger sisters that a publisher contacted me about my novel posted on Shosetsuka ni Naro, a user-generated novel-publishing site, and to my surprise, one of them revealed that she also posts her writings there! Without letting on that she was writing anything, she had actually completed a novel! I read it and thought the story was fantastic, and her female characters were totally cute. She was writing a lot and quickly, not leaving her stories unfinished like someone else... Publishers should've reached out to her first! I could see her first book coming out before mine... but it took a few years before that happened, hee-hee.

My novel finally landed on the shelves, though! It's been so long since the publishing company first told me they wanted to publish it, and it actually happening, that somehow it hasn't really hit me yet that I'm now a published author. I awaited the release day still not quite believing that it was *my* book coming out in print, but at least I was thrilled to see Miho Takeoka's gorgeously cute illustrations, which made me squeal with delight.

I'll try to follow up with a sequel before too many years go by...! Stay tuned for *Maiden of the Needle*, Vol. 2!